From the Flames

To Eudene,
God Bless you!
Hannah Rose
Duggan
Psalm 37:4

From the Flames

HANNAH ROSE DUGGAN

WestBow
PRESS
A DIVISION OF THOMAS NELSON

WestBow Press books may be ordered through booksellers or by contacting:

WestBow Press
A Division of Thomas Nelson
1663 Liberty Drive
Bloomington, IN 47403
www.westbowpress.com
1-(866) 928-1240

Because of the dynamic nature of the Internet, any web addresses or
links contained in this book may have changed since publication and
may no longer be valid. The views expressed in this work are solely those
of the author and do not necessarily reflect the views of the publisher,
and the publisher hereby disclaims any responsibility for them.

Certain stock imagery © Thinkstock.
Any people depicted in stock imagery provided by Thinkstock are models,
and such images are being used for illustrative purposes only.

ISBN: 978-1-4497-8240-5 (e)
ISBN: 978-1-4497-8239-9 (sc)
ISBN: 978-1-4497-8238-2 (hc)

Library of Congress Control Number: 2013900825

Printed in the United States of America

WestBow Press rev. date: 2/18/2013

To my Mom and Dad,
For loving me, letting me dream big,
And treating every story I've ever written like a Masterpiece
I love you guys!

You've gone so far away,

my darling, Gone so far away

The ships, the sails have stolen you,

have snatched you from my gaze

Ne'er was a goodbye e'er so short,

Nor a kiss so sweet

I'll pray for you, I'll wait for

you, until again we meet

And when you are alone,

my darling, when you are alone

If storms and troubles take you

, lead you far away from home

I pray that angels light the sky,

to shine upon the sea

And God Himself will guide you,

and bring you back to me

And when you are afraid,

my darling, when you are afraid

If worry claims you for her own,

if darkness shrieks your name

Take courage, then, my dearest love,

for though you cannot see

Our God is watching o'er you,

He'll bring you back to me

And when we meet again,

my darling, when we meet again

Although it be on distant shores,

where life has met its end

No sweeter joy shall find my hear,

no day will greater be

I'll thank the God, Who found us

both, Who brought you back to me

I'll thank the God, Who found us

both, Who brought you back to me

Chapter 1

He was dead, or nearly so. Had you asked me that very morning, I surely would have told you that hardly anyone ever came to our cottage in the woods. He was half buried in the snow. How long had he been there? It had been snowing for days. There it was; a vapor of breath, weaving then disappearing just in front of the stranger's face. It was at that moment that the full fury of my fear came to life. I sprang from my spot as one whipped, knowing that my swiftness to act could be the difference between life and death for this man. My chest began to thrash with a terrified pounding as if to the rhythm in my thoughts. *Life or death. Life or death.* I dashed for the house and just before I reached it, glanced back over my shoulder. Through the veil of white, I could just see it; the dark blur of something huddled, dying in the snow, and for one moment, I wished this were all just a dream.

When my mother saw me just inside the door, she rushed to me. "Elizabeth!" she exclaimed. "Where have you been?" the question was not angry, but I knew I had worried her.

"Mother, there is someone in the snow!" I gasped.

"What?" her brow crinkled with concern.

"A traveler. He must have been caught in the storm. I have never seen him before."

I did not have to ask. She moved to the window and peered out, pressing her fingers against the glass. She looked for several moments, but I could tell by the way her eyes narrowed at me that she had only seen the usual landscape. I pushed toward the window and gazed out. Nothing. The yard was empty. There was no dark blur blotting the snow, and I began to question my own memory. What I had seen not two minutes before was now gone.

"Bethy?" she waited for an explanation.

"I promise you, Mother! I saw him."

She placed a work worn hand on my shoulder. "Of course you saw something, but the snow plays tricks on our minds. It was probably an animal."

"But I saw a face!" I shuddered at the remembrance. "It was pale and dying."

She bit her lower lip in indecision. "I'm sorry, Bethy. I don't see anything."

I burned at the thought of my own mother not believing me at my word. Yet, I was beginning to doubt it myself. I noticed the fear in her dark eyes, saw the untimely threads of gray straying from her ebony braid, and remembered all that she had endured in the last year. Shame overtook me at having worried her.

"I'm sorry." I stared at the ground, subdued. "It was probably just—"

With a crash the door blew open. I looked to see my father tread across the threshold. I thought his footsteps sounded heavy when I realized he was not alone. He supported the lifeless form of the stranger with the man's arm stretched across my father's shoulders. Mother rushed over to him, but I didn't move. So, I had seen someone. Yet, at the first test of confidence I had denied my own eyes. I was sick as the realization dawned on me that if Father had not seen him his life would have been lost, and it would have been no one's fault but mine.

"Bethy, ready a place by the fire." my mother's commanding voice brought me out of my thoughts. I did as she asked, setting one of her hand-made quilts by the fire. My father said not a word, but laid the man down and knelt there inspecting his eyes, hands, and feet. Father's fingers never rested but moved in that skilled way of his. I watched him for some time, my eyes following his hands. After several minutes Mother coughed to get my attention, and when she had caught my eye nodded to the other room. "I'll help your father. You get to bed."

I nodded, feeling disappointed. Yet, my eyelids began to droop. All at once, I did not care what Father was doing. All I wanted was to sleep and be relieved of all thought until morning. I turned to leave, but as I did my father's voice caught my ear. "Beth."

"Yes, Father?" I yawned.

"I need your help." he said, without looking up.

Everything in me groaned, and I looked to my mother imploring.

"John, our Bethy needs her rest. I will be glad to—"

"Katherine, I must have her do this."

A look passed between them that I was too weary to interpret. My mother broke the gaze and stepped over the stranger as if to move past me into the other room; instead, she leaned close to me. "Do as your father bids, Dear." Planting a warm kiss on my cheek she passed through the curtain that divided the two rooms.

I cast a tired glance toward the fire, and knelt next to my father who was binding one of the stranger's frostbitten hands.

As I sat down, he hardly seemed to notice me. It was a strange thing that he would ask for my help since I had never given assistance in his practice before.

"Not a day of work." he observed motioning to the palm of the stranger's blackened hand.

"Do you believe he is wealthy?" I asked.

"I cannot say." He continued to bind with the skill that only experience provides. Finishing, he looked up at me. "Were you watching?"

I nodded. It was a lie.

"Alright then, you do the other hand." He held out one of the bandages to me, but I hesitated.

"Don't be afraid."

His voice stirred me. When I looked up, his eyes caught mine, and held them until something which had been shaken in me steadied. I bound the other hand as well as I could while Father

4

gently adjusted my inexperienced hands here and there. I dare say he probably had to redo my work later that night. When I had finished, he looked at me in that same unblinking way. "Fine." he said in a whisper that reflected the soft firelight. His approval made me feel nervous and even uncomfortable. I looked away, unsure of what to do. He reached for my hand and held it so firmly that my fingertips began to sting. "Elizabeth." His voice was low but resolute. "Do you blame yourself for your brother's death?"

I was stunned. It had been nearly a year. I could not answer, but he understood my silence possibly more than me.

"Perhaps," he paused for moment, tapping his fingers together just in front of his face. "Perhaps I have been remiss by you."

I wanted to question, but he held up his hand and continued, "I have not taught you as I should have. I was so concerned that your brother had a trade that I did not teach you what little I knew. Perhaps, if I had..." He cleared his throat, but didn't finish.

My heart was breaking for him. I loved him so, and it was painful to watch him suffer like this.

"Off you go then." He looked away from me at last, and I was relieved that he did not continue. I stood, bid him goodnight, and I wearily crept into the next room. There was my mother, not yet asleep I knew. More likely than not, she had listened to our conversation.

I lay down on my straw-filled mattress, bewildered by what had just happened. I had not heard my father mention my brother once since we dug the little plot in the graveyard. Yes, it had been my fault.

—m—

He wasn't even seven, and yet the life was fading on his face. I begged him not to leave me. I needed him. And yet, he slipped further and further beyond my grasp. A brief look, a final smile, a short-lived breath, and he was gone. No, not again. I could not lose him again. My head was buried in the quilts covering his little body when someone shook my shoulder. "No!" I protested to whomever was trying to pull me away from him. "No, leave me be."

"Elizabeth!" I recognized my father's voice. I lifted my head from the quilt to find myself, not at any deathbed, but grasping my own quilts, in the throes of a nightmare. My face was wet, and my chest still heaved from crying.

"Are you well?" he asked, ill at ease.

"It was just a dream." But even at the words, my heart convulsed. It had not just been a dream.

"I must go out." my father whispered in the dark. "Henry Denton was here. Seems his mother has had a fall. You will stay here won't you, and mind things?"

I knew what he meant, but the thought frightened me. I wanted to protest, but I had a sudden remembrance of his words the night before and stayed my tongue.

I pushed myself to my feet, and he turned to leave. Yet as he reached the curtain I felt a rush of panic. "Wait!" It was louder than I had meant it to be. I looked at the tranquil form of my mother still in undisturbed slumber.

Father turned back and read it all on my face. "I trust you, Bethy." One of his rare smiles appeared then, and he left. So it was not with any confidence of mine but in obedience that I dressed and went into the next room as my father shut the front door behind him. Sitting on the old chair he had made for Mother years ago, I tried to block out the images of my dream, without success. They weren't just pictures my mind had created. They were memories, wretched memories that would never leave. The fever had taken many in our village last winter. Father had never been home. He was always with the sick. He had never truly been trained as a physician, but what little he knew he used to help the people in our village. He was the closest thing Tonbridge had to a doctor. The only other people willing to take in the ill were Lord and Lady Garret. The couple lived with their daughter in Garret Hall, an inherited mansion, and they would not turn away the sick. The fever was almost gone, the danger nearly over, when Lady Garret fell ill. Both my parents went that night. They left not knowing how the illness has slithered its way into our home. Lady Garret had died before my parents reached her, but the snow kept them at Garret Hall for three days. They returned to find me alone in the dark bent over the body of my brother. That day would never leave me.

I stared at the stranger by our fire. I looked long and hard at his face, guessing him to be seven or eight years older than I, perhaps a few years past twenty. There was something about him that was so distinct. His fair hair and the structure of his face all seemed so familiar.

Shivering, I glanced out the window. The sky was still black with no sign of dawn, and I wondered how early it was. The storm, however, had stopped, and I could see the snow in even white sheets on the ground. I nestled myself deeper into the chair. As it rocked back and forth, the rhythmic squeak and groan was comforting. This job was not such an unpleasant one after all. Squeak, Groan… No, I believed I could stay here for… forever. Squeak, Groan…

—⁂—

A chill woke me. In the dreary light of day seeping through the window, I found myself staring into eyes that I would never forget. The first thing that struck me was their color. Blue was not the word. They were nearly white, like the light that is only seen for a fleeting instant when you first strike a fire. They stared at me so unblinkingly that, for a moment, I wondered if he were one of those odd fellows who slept with their eyes open. I'd heard of such things, though I'd never believed them. Yet, as I stood and stoked the fire they followed me. He tried to move his lips as if to form words. I noticed how dry and cracked they were. Seeing that my father had left a jug of water nearby, I fetched a cloth and dabbed some of the moisture onto his lips. "Where am I?" His voice cracked above a whisper.

"The Atlee Cottage." I answered.

"John, and Katherine Atlee?"

"Yes." I gave him a sideways look, placing the water jug on a shelf.

A light dawned in those unnerving eyes, and he turned his head to look at me. "You're Elizabeth."

I froze, unable to face him. "Yes, I'm Miss Atlee."

"Dei, gratia." he whispered.

Turning to look at him, I suddenly wished that my father were home. It crossed my mind that I might be dealing with a madman.

His eyes caught mine again. They were shining. "You are the answer to my prayers, Miss Atlee. You see, you are the reason I'm here. I've come in search of you."

Chapter 2

I was unable to move, rigid in my spot. "What did you say?" I asked, trying to search his face.

He laughed, seeming oblivious to my reaction. "I never thought I would find you."

I took two steps forward, trying not to let my hands shake as I folded them behind my back. "Who are you?" I asked slowly.

His face relaxed into a smile. "My name is Peter."

The door crashed closed behind me, and I spun around to see my father with snow still melting in flakes on his clothing. He stood solemn and motionless. His eyes were locked with those of the stranger. Travelling upward, his gaze searched mine then moved again to the other man's face.

"Elizabeth." he said without even glancing up at me. "The fire is dying. Fetch some wood for it, won't you?"

"Yes, Father." I answered in a whisper. By the time I had snatched my shawl off of its hook and hurried out the door, I realized my heart was pounding. My hands trembled slightly as I gathered up the wood. Father's attempt at sending me away had been poorly disguised, but I did not hold it against him. On the contrary, I was relieved to have escaped. As I neared the house, with wood in hand, I heard my father's voice. My hand was on the door when I heard my father's words, low but forceful.

"I want not one word of this to her. Do you understand me?"

I pushed the door open. My father's back was to me, and he had not noticed my presence, so intent was he on an answer from the young man in front of him. My eyes again met with the stranger. The room was still. His eyes looked into mine, more than ever resembling translucent flames. His stare pleaded with me. For what, I could not guess. Finally, the eyes shut in painful resolve. "I understand."

The wind slammed the door behind me, and Father turned, but would not meet my eye. Dropping the wood in its box with a clatter, I waited for a response, an explanation, a look, anything, but both men remained silent.

—⚡—

The pressure only increased as the day wore on. Each of us was as tense as a bow string ready to release. I was asked to leave the house several times, and each time was more contrived and frustrating than the last. I asked questions and received no answers. The stranger said nothing when I was in the house. In the entire course of the morning, I learned only two things from my mother and Father; His name was Peter Lockton, and he came from Oxford, at the university. When anything further than that was brought up, the subject was changed. By late afternoon Mother sent me out to collect the eggs for the second time that day. It became clear that if this went on any longer one of our bow strings was going to snap, and it was going to be mine.

I made my way around the henhouse, toward the barn. Frustrated as I was, there was something else on my mind. Though it was easy to be angry when in the house, the moment I was alone, something inside of me began to stir. It was a feeling that had only come upon me once or twice before. It made my heart rush and took my breath away. It was music. Nothing I could hear, but it was there, haunting me as it did from time to time.

It hadn't been like this before, only in the last year. We had held my brother's funeral the same day as Lady Garret's. It was one of the most miserable days of my life. Yet it was that day I met Sybil Garret. Before her mother died, I had never liked her, but that day things had changed. Our broken hearts found one another in the graveyard, and I still counted her as my closest friend. Once, she had shown me an instrument of her mother's. It was polished and carved in the shape of an hourglass. She showed me how to hold it with the lower end tucked under my chin. She let me hold the bow, and taught me how to draw it across the strings. As I did, my heart raced. That beautiful sound had come from me, from my fingers. It had moved, and flowed with a will of its own. Sybil had called it "amazing", asking where I had learned. The truth was, I hadn't learned. I hadn't even seen such an instrument before. Never would I forget the way she looked at me with her green eyes flashing. "Then it's not just amazing." she'd said. "It's a gift from God."

If it was a gift, it was a forbidden one. I knew the day I played, that it would be the first and last time. According to my uncle, the village priest, all music outside of the church was evil. I tried to fight the melody that would come over me, but I could not. That day when the bow had come off of the strings the playing ended forever, but the music was with me still.

"Bethy, what are you doing in here?"

I spun around to see my mother in the stable doorway. I hadn't meant to end up in the stable, but there was really nowhere else to go.

"I thought I sent you to fetch the eggs." she said.

"I got them this morning." I answered, staring down at my shoes.

She seated herself in the pile of clean straw near the door, folding her hands in her lap. "Perhaps we ought to talk."

I sat down next to her, searching her face.

"I'm sorry it's been this way today."

"I'm sorry my presence is such a burden." I sighed.

"It's not you. Truly, it isn't. Your father's just trying to protect you. It's his job."

"Is the man dangerous?" I asked.

"No. Not that we know of."

"Why is he here?"

She bit her lip. Silence.

I cleared my throat. "How long will he stay?"

"Well, your father needs an apprentice."

"An apprentice?"

"We've always talked about it."

"And he's always been against it."

"Well, things are different now."

"Why?" I cried.

The silence was deafening. "I'm sorry, Bethy. Some things are better left unsaid."

"Don't misunderstand." I said, softening my tone. "I'm not angry at Master Lockton. I just don't want every day to be like this one."

"It won't. I promise."

I looked at the ground, unsure of whether or not to believe her.

"Bethy." Her shaky hand rested on my shoulder. "Please, don't push me away. I can't bear it. I've already lost my stillborn baby, and my boy. I can't lose you too."

I turned and embraced her. "You won't. I promise."

—◦◦◦—

I had never liked our extra room. It had once been where my father had kept his medical patients. It was in this room that my brother had breathed his last. Now, it was Master Lockton's room, but as I stood in the doorway I saw that there was no sign of Master Lockton.

Footsteps sounded behind me, and I spun around to see him, realizing just how meddlesome I looked. "I'm sorry." I said, hurriedly moving toward the door way.

He stepped aside, but I paused at the door. "It's time to leave for Mass. I was told to come and get you. I apologize for the intrusion."

"So do I." he offered.

Silence hung in the air.

"Miss Atlee." he began slowly. "Frightening and angering you was never my intention."

I studied Master Lockton. In the past three days, he had recovered quite well, and was beginning to settle into our home.

"I wish to repay you." he continued.

My eyes were fixed on his face. "How?"

"I would like to teach you to write. That is if you want to learn."

My mouth fell open. "No." I gasped. "No thank you." I pushed past him, nearly knocking my mother over as she came in.

"Bethy, I thought I told you to fetch Master Lockton." She shot a glance in his direction, to which he gave a slight nod.

"Good Day, Mrs. Atlee." he greeted.

"Good day." She searched my face as her eyes narrowed. "We're leaving for Mass. Master Lockton, would you like to attend with us?"

—ᴍ—

Never was evening Mass so hard to endure. My uncle, who usually did the service, was visiting another perish for the next few months. Instead, a man I had never seen before got up, and performed the needed services. I, however, was unable to concentrate. Covertly, I continued to stare at our guest, wondering if he had attended Mass wherever he was from. Indeed, I could find no fault except that his eyes remained closed for most of the service, which made watching him quite convenient.

After the service was over, Sybil Garret caught me by the arm, her red curls in a flurry. "I must speak with you."

"Of course." I stepped outside the chapel with her.

"How long has he been here?" she asked, when we were outside.

"About three days." I watched her face twist and struggle as if trying to understand. "Sybil, do you know him?"

She nodded, her lips forming a thin line.

"Is he dangerous?"

"No!" she cried, as though I had just suggested murder. "Of course not, but," she hesitated. "Elizabeth, do you know why he's here?"

"No one will tell me."

"I see."

"He wants to give me writing lessons."

She turned to face me. "You're going to take them aren't you?"

"Of course not! Why would I?"

She crossed her arms. "Elizabeth Atlee! Master Peter Lockton was one of the best students at Oxford University, and he wants to teach you. Why wouldn't you?"

I let my gaze slip downward.

"Elizabeth." she spoke slowly. "Are you afraid of looking like a fool?"

"Well, who isn't?"

She placed a hand, under my chin, and tilted my face upward. "You could do this and be good at it."

I pulled away. "But something's not right. He said he was here to find me. I don't know why he was searching for me, but I wish he would just go home."

"Don't say that." Her breath frosted the air in front of her, her green eyes flashing like a terrified animal's.

"Sybil." I urged in a low tone. "What do you know?"

She held up her hands and stepped backward. "Not very much."

"Please tell me." I begged, breathlessly.

"I can't. Not here."

"Where then?"

"We need to be alone." Her voice shook.

"Elizabeth!" my mother called from inside the church. "We're leaving."

"I'll follow. You go ahead." I called back to her.

"No, I don't want you out in this night air."

"Yes, Mother." I looked back to Sybil. "I'll come tomorrow."

She gripped my fingers with an icy hand. "Elizabeth, tomorrow will be too late."

"What else do you want me to do?" I hissed.

She stepped back, looking hurt.

"I'll come early." I promised as I turned to go.

"Elizabeth." Her voice was warning.

I turned back to her.

"Take the lessons."

"I need to go." I pulled away and hurried up the steps to the chapel. Once more, I glanced over my shoulder.

She held up her hand, and her lips moved as she whispered, "Goodbye."

Chapter 3

"Sybil is gone."

"Gone?" I stared at Lord Garret. The early morning light made the lines of grief on his face all too visible.

"Yes, she is headed to London for a finishing school."

"She never said anything." I said, feeling dazed.

"Yes, well, I told her not mention it to anyone. I dislike the politics of this area. I wish to move to the city all together, but I have obligations. It's better for her there right now."

"Then, she won't be coming back?"

"Not for some time. She left something for you though."

He stepped inside and returned with a piece of parchment in his hand. Holding it forth, he motioned for me to take it. I reached out, but he would not release it. Leaning forward, he whispered to me, "Be not forgetful to entertain strangers, for some have entertained angels without knowing." With that, he released his hold on the letter, and I stepped back.

"Thank you?" I hesitated.

"Well, I'm just sorry she cannot talk to you in person, but perhaps she will be back with the warm weather."

I nodded and escaped down the path. I looked at the parchment. It was a drawing of the instrument I had played that day. I didn't need her to interpret it. She had sent me the same message the night before. *"Take the lessons."* Maybe I would, for her. I walked mindlessly down the hill toward our cottage, but I didn't want to go home. I wanted to be alone. I wanted to think. Outside the village, I stopped and snapped a twig from one of the trees. I had an impulse to hurl it as far as I could into the snow, or crack it into splinters. I stared down at it when an idea came to me. Bending down, I tried to keep my knees out of the powdery snow. With the sharper end of the twig, I made little impressions in the whiteness, sketching lines, poking dents, and brushing patterns into a glistening picture.

"More Bethy. Draw more."

I could hear his laughing voice calling me from years away. I had entertained my brother for hours with my drawings. Sweeping my stick pen over the frosty ground, I found myself smiling. As I put the finishing touches on my sketch, I looked up to the clouded skies and hoped, as I often did, that there was Someone up there to talk to. Not the God my uncle talked about. Uncle Jacob was sure to let me know that 'That Someone' hated me, and had hated me ever since my brother died. No, the Someone I searched for knew that it wasn't my fault, knew how I felt about my brother, about Sybil, about everything. That Someone was in the music that haunted and pursued me. That Someone was in Sybil's laugh, and in the sunset over the mountains in summer. That Someone understood, and I wouldn't give up believing that somehow maybe my brother was with that Someone.

I stepped back from my drawing. "What do you think of that?" I laughed, pulling loose strands of hair from my face.

"I think it's lovely." a voice said behind me.

My heart dropped. Spinning around, I saw Master Lockton, and had the urge to run.

"I'm sorry." He held up his hands. "I didn't mean to frighten you."

I stared at the ground.

"Ever." he added.

Without glancing up, I nodded.

He stepped around me to take a closer look at my drawing. "This is beautiful."

"It's nothing." I said, smothering it with my foot. "I mean, it's not very good."

He was watching me, with flaming eyes. "I would disagree."

My breath appeared in worried little clouds. "What are you doing out here?" I finally asked.

"Your mother fears a storm is on its way. She sent me to get you."

I nodded and hurried down the path toward home.

He caught up with me. "I truly didn't mean to scare you."

"I know." I glanced up at him, and I saw it. Whatever it was that filled me with music and blessed Sybil with laughter was in

Peter Lockton's stare. If there was a Someone Who cared, Master Lockton knew where to find Him.

We had climbed the hill toward home, and he stopped in front of the targets my father used for his shooting practice. "How long have you been drawing?"

I let out a deep breath. "I haven't drawn since my brother died. He was the only one I ever drew for." A cheerless smile crossed my face. "He loved it. I suppose I feel guilty doing it without him." I gazed at the little graveyard on the hill. "No one truly understands unless they've lost someone they love." I stopped, wondering why all of this was spilling out. I looked at him, but he too was focused on the cemetery.

"When I was seven, I lost both my parents." The pain in his voice was palpable. "Maybe that's why I like to see you with yours."

"Master Lockton." I said.

He seemed to waken from his thoughtful state, and turned again to me.

I stared at the ground, and my voice shook a bit. "Is writing anything like drawing?"

He closed his eyes and nodded. "Very much so."

"Then," I swallowed the dryness in my throat. "I think I'd like to learn."

"Then, I think I'd like to teach you." He beamed. "And it's Peter if you don't mind."

—⁂—

We began lessons the next afternoon when Master Lockton had finished helping my father with his rounds in the village. We sat at the table in the sitting room while my mother sewed in the next room.

The lesson began with the alphabet. Peter taught me to trace it and write it. I was quite proficient at copying, but no matter how much he said it or how often he quizzed me, I couldn't remember a single one by name. When Mother called me to help prepare the evening meal I went gratefully. Peter said I did a splendid job, but I didn't believe him. I was horrible at this. What good would any of this be if I couldn't remember even the names and sounds of the letters? Yet, I promised to give myself a week, and if I had learned nothing, the lessons would stop.

The next day Peter was late in coming. I fetched a piece of material since parchment was too expensive for practice. While I waited, I noticed that the ink had been left on the table along with the quill pen. I uncapped the ink and dipped the pen in it. I scribbled out my alphabet on the cloth, and finished just as he came in. He apologized for his tardiness then noticed my work.

"Where did you get this?" he asked, examining the cloth in my hands.

"I wrote it."

He picked it up and gazed at it. "But what did you copy?"

"Nothing. Did I do something wrong?"

He set it on the table and stared at it perplexed, then looked back up at me. "You wrote this entirely from memory?"

I nodded.

"I want to try a new exercise." He picked up another piece of material from the table and scrawled the letters, out of order. He then set it in front of me. "Trace it first."

I traced the letters, and he took away the sheet. "Now, write them, without looking."

I looked at him in disbelief, but he prompted me to continue. So, I closed my eyes for a moment, took a deep breath, and wrote; *D Y b C T A g.* I bit the inside of my lip, trying to remember. *Z N d X a p H.*

When I reached the end, he took it from me and studied it, pacing back and forth. The silence made me nervous.

"Is it right?" I asked, finally.

He compared the two sheets and looked up at me. "It's perfect."

I smiled at my accomplishment, but he shook his head. "I don't understand. How do you do that?"

"Do what?"

He sighed, and I was worried that I had displeased him. "Miss Atlee, I have seen many people write. Believe me when I tell you that there are brilliant scholars who can't do what you just showed me."

"Write their alphabet?" I raised one eyebrow.

"No." he laughed. "Memorize it so quickly! You just traced this sequence of letters once, yet you could rewrite it without looking."

"You mean, it's special?"

"Very special!" His face was bright with excitement. "In fact, it's extraordinary."

I stared at the characters staining the cloth. "But I can't tell you what those letters are, or what they say."

"Then, that's what we'll work on next."

True to his word, we spent the next three days learning the names and sounds. I found that having a trick for each one helped me to memorize it. *A* was at an *Angle*. *M* had *More* points than *N*. Simple things helped me master the letters and sounds. There was one letter that I couldn't find a trick for, no matter how hard I tried. When I told Peter this, he laughed and pointed at the letter. "This is an *E*, and it begins a very important word."

"What?"

With a secretive smile, he scratched something down on the parchment in his hand and set it on the table. "This word."

It was lovely. The lines flowed over the page and spun into thin little ribbons of meaning. "What is it?" I wondered.

"Elizabeth." He grinned.

I started when he said my name, then, realized that he was motioning toward the page. "My name?"

"Yes." He nodded.

Timidly, I reached out and touched the surface. "May I, may I keep this?"

Again, he nodded, and I snatched it up. It was beautiful.

I learned to write much quicker than Peter had expected. Not only that, but once I was able to memorize letters and words, I could remember and repeat anything I wrote. Peter became part of our family. He brought a lightness back into the house which none of has known for quite some time. My father's steps were lighter. My mother smiled again. It was very much like having a brother again. My own brother had been eight years younger than I, and Peter was eight years older.

Writing freed me, just like the music. It was an imperceptible joy that filled me when a quill was in my hand.

Peter was with us every day, except when my father needed no help. On those days, he would leave with his satchel at dawn, and return at dusk. Once I saw the pages that fell out of his satchel. There was writing on every single one, but I couldn't read them. They were in Latin, just like the Bible at the front of the chapel. I stayed my curiosity and kept my questions. The only thing I dared ask was what he did on those days when he disappeared.

"I write the truth." he answered.

I didn't need to ask any more questions. Peter probably hoped I didn't know what he meant, but I did. One could not grow up with a priest in your family without hearing about those who believed that the Scriptures ought to be written in English rather than in Latin. These people were excommunicated and imprisoned as seditious heretics and rebels. "Peter, that's forbidden."

"I know." He nodded.

"Then why are you doing it?"

"Because the people need to know the truth. Just because something is forbidden, doesn't mean it's wrong."

"But it's against the law."

"Men's laws, not God's."

"What are God's laws then?" I challenged.

Peter looked at me solemnly. "No one will know unless they

understand what the Word of God says. It's His Words that set people free."

I struggled over the decision of whether or not to tell my parents of my discovery, but to my astonishment, they already knew. They had made a deal with Peter that he could continue his work as long as it was not in our home. Peter obeyed this, and life went on.

—∞—

Spring came and went, giving way to a green summer. I hoped it would never end, and that we would go on and on as we were. Oh, that we were born to a world like that! Yet, we are not. We are born here, where things seldom stay the same for long.

Chapter 4

"Bethy?" My mother walked into our writing lesson. "We need to leave early for Mass this evening."

"Why?" I asked as she collected her shawl with my father just behind.

Father pulled his hat down tightly. "Your uncle is back in the village, and we would like to have a few words with him."

I gathered my shawl, and the four of us stepped out into the frozen twilight.

When we reached the village, Mother and Father asked to speak to my uncle, alone. The rectory was connected to the chapel with a door leading in between. A maid answered my father's knock, and showed them in, closing the door behind them.

"May we go into the chapel?" Peter asked me.

"As long as we ask the caretaker."

Tonbridge's chapel had several different men who worked at its upkeep, taking turns throughout the month. Today, there was a man whom I had never seen before. He towered over the pews, the duster in his hand looking like a fragile twig. At seeing him, Peter's eyes grew wide. "Stay here." he told me.

I sighed, but he didn't notice. He crept up behind the man as he dusted the church for service. "Isaac Colt." Peter's voice rang clearly through the sanctuary. "I never thought I'd see you again, but least of all here."

Dropping his duster, the man froze and stared at my teacher. "Peter?"

The two laughed, and the man gripped Peter in a crushing embrace. "You fool!" he said, stepping back. "I thought you were dead! Why didn't you send us word?"

The voices grew quiet, so I edged nearer to the door.

"Does she know?" the caretaker's voice boomed.

"No." he was quick to reply. "I was so close. It's just not His timing."

"Indeed."

"Isaac." Peter said in a hushed tone. "I need your help with something."

"Anything."

"I've been translating the Psalms. I acquired the Latin transcripts, and I've been working through it on my own."

"Did Master Wycliffe assign this to you?" The man sounded confused.

"No. Why?"

The caretaker laughed. "Because he gave *me* the task of translating the Psalms just before I left, but I need your help to write them. That's part of the reason I've come to find you."

I heard their steps nearing the door, and I backed away. Seconds later they were in the doorway, and I heard Peter call me.

"Miss Elizabeth Atlee, Isaac Colt."

"Pleasure." Master Colt nodded politely.

I studied him. He must have been near the age of my father, perhaps a bit younger, and much taller. Peter looked like a child, standing next to him. His hands, I noticed, were scarred, and dark, as though they had once been burned.

"You're quite welcome in the chapel." he told Peter. "Service starts within the hour."

"Thank you." Peter turned to me as his friend stepped back inside. "I want to show you something."

I followed him into the darkened room, and blinked, waiting for my eyes to adjust. It was the chapel I had been baptized and raised in. Nothing ever changed. The altar, the pews, the candles, they all remained the same. Peter headed up the aisle to where my uncle led the service. "This is it." he whispered, motioning to an enormous book. "Do you know what this is?"

"It's a Bible." I answered.

"Yes, do you know what language it's written in?"

"Latin." I said, without missing a moment.

"Very good. Now, why do you think this is written in Latin?"

"I don't know. I can't understand it."

"Exactly." A deep sigh escaped my teacher. "But, if you could, you would be reading the words of God. Think of it. How different would men be if they could read the words of their Maker?"

My heart sank. "Then, you mean to say, that you believe in the same God as my uncle."

A shadow passed over his face. "Miss Atlee, I don't claim to know what it is that your uncle believes, but I will tell you this. The God in this book loves His children. He does not blame them for what they did not do. He knows that they make mistakes, and He has forgiven them. Does that sound like the God of your uncle?"

I was opening my mouth to speak, when I saw in the reflection of a golden candlestick, the door to the rectory opening. "Oh, no!" I breathed, just as my uncle's voice boomed from the back.

"What do you think you're doing?"

We both turned to see, the illustrious Father Jacob Chancley, fuming, red faced, and fluttering up the aisle in all of his priestly garb, like a fat, enraged crow.

"How dare you touch those things! Who let you two in?" he sputtered. "Colt!"

Isaac Colt stepped calmly in from the doorway. "Yes, Sir?"

"Did you let these two… two…" He searched for a word. He couldn't find one.

"I let them in, Sir."

"But why?"

"Because this is a chapel, Sir, not a palace. And, I am a caretaker, not the troll who locks your gates for you." His composure infuriated my uncle.

The priest made a sound of disgust. "You are relieved of

your position here. I don't care if you are my Bishop's son. I should have known better than to let you in! Men like you never change."

"As you wish." He bowed slightly, without taking his eyes off of the priest's. He nodded to Peter then stepped outside through the chapel doors.

As my uncle turned to us, Peter stepped in front of me. "This was my fault, Father Chancley."

I could tell by the hatred in the cleric's gaze that this was not the first time he and Peter had met. "You think you're terribly clever, don't you? Coming here, pretending that you're not the son of a filthy heretic! You left several holes in your story to the Atlee's, didn't you?"

"Well, I assumed that you had filled them in long before my arrival."

"Get out!" he raged.

Peter didn't move.

The priest stepped forward until he was standing right over the younger man. "I can see to it that all of your searching was for nothing."

Peter's looked at me with panic in his eyes. All color drained from his features. He writhed with indecision, and then nodded. "I'll go."

"Peter!" I started, but he took no notice of me.

Father Chancley grinned. "Then, we understand one another?"

"Perfectly." Peter said with his jaw tight.

"Good." The cleric moved out of the aisle to let Peter walk by.

My teacher turned to me, and I noticed tears in the corners of his eyes. "Good day, Miss Atlee." Within moments, Peter was out the door.

"And as for you, Elizabeth, be thankful your parents got to me in time. Don't let him fool any of you. He is a thief who has come to steal the hearts of the faithful." With a satisfied smile, he turned to go.

"You're wrong." I answered.

He halted. "I beg your pardon?"

My voice was calm and even. "Peter Lockton is a respectable man, and my parents are happy to have him. You have no right to—"

"I have every right!" he shrieked. "You don't know who this man is. Keep him under your roof, and you'll see how much ill will he brings you. He's accursed just like his father before him! He's already begun to poison you! I can see it. Just listen to the way you're talking."

"I meant no disrespect."

"Then you will be silent." His gaze held mine. Neither of us willing to back down.

The rectory door slammed shut behind my parents as they entered the chapel. I saw my mother's face. She was begging me not to speak, silently pleading for me to stay out of trouble. I looked once again on my uncle, and couldn't stop the words from coming. "You will not steal this from me too." Pushing past him, I bolted from the church. I saw Peter standing on the edge of the street.

"Peter!" I called, running up next to him. "You can't leave."

He turned to look down at me. "I have to go."

"Why?"

The angry tears formed again. "If I don't, Chancley is going see that I regret it."

"But what could he do to you?"

He looked me in the eye. "He could hurt you."

I was appalled. "But he wouldn't! He's just angry that we were in the chapel."

"He is angry." Peter agreed, smiling bitterly. "He's angry that I made it this far and that I'm not dead as he had hoped."

"You just don't understand him."

"I wish I didn't." he sighed. "Chancley has taken everything from me. Don't think that he'll stop now, just because you're his niece." He closed his eyes as if remembering. "He'd do anything."

Chapter 5

When morning came, I woke to find that my parents had finally gone to bed. Their discussion with Peter had lasted most of night, and though their voices kept me up I couldn't make out any words. I dressed and slipped into the front room. The curtain to Peter's room was wide open. He was gone. I poked the dying embers of the fire, when I noticed his satchel, on the hearth, and picked it up. How could he have forgotten the only thing he owned? Looking out the window, I wondered when he had gone. As I gazed out, I saw someone in the gray light. It was him. Fetching my shawl, I threw the door open and rushed outside. I halted several steps from him.

"It's a bit early to be up, isn't it?" he asked, without turning to face me.

I threaded the satchel's strap through my fingers. "You're going to need this if you're leaving."

"I don't want to. I shouldn't have stayed here. I shouldn't have come in the first place. I just had to know."

"Peter, I still don't know why you came, but I'm thankful that you did. This family will never be the same, but none of us regrets your coming."

He turned to look at me. "Not yet." He took the satchel from me and slung it over his shoulder.

"There must be something we can do."

"There is." He dug into his satchel, and pulled out several pages, folded and sealed. As he handed them to me, there was a look in his eyes that made me feel as though I had just been handed the crown. "Guard it. Protect it. Keep it."

"I will." I promised. "Will we ever see you again?"

"Dei Gratia." With a slight bow, he turned and walked down the dirt path in the late summer light, past the stable and disappeared from view into the dark trees.

—✼—

I pealed the seal back and opened the folded pages. Something fell out and hit the floor. Picking it up, I saw that it was a pendant and chain. I dusted it off and studied it in the firelight. It was a delicate gold leaf. Never in my life had I held anything so beautiful. It glinted in the light and stole my breath away. The pages were a letter from Peter, written on the back of some of the Latin transcripts I had found before.

"Elizabeth,

"I know that you search for what is true and right. I pray that God brings someone to teach you now that I cannot. Don't stop

searching. If you don't know where to find God, know that He is close to the broken hearted. He has been pursuing you since the day you were born. He is in that secret place of your heart, the place where you think you are most alone. He's there, waiting, calling you with His music."

I stopped reading. Music. How could Peter have known? Never had I told anyone. I continued to read.

"The necklace is an extraordinarily special piece. My father was a goldsmith. This was the last piece that he created before he died. I hope you wear it, and treasure it. Elizabeth, take courage and be strong."

The rest of the pages were blank on the back, except for the last one, which read: *"Tell Colt, you have what he's looking for."*

I lay staring at the ceiling. The even breathing of my parents told me that I was the only one still awake. I had given up on sleep hours ago, but I could not stop the thoughts and questions from tumbling over and over in my mind. He had been gone for two days. I didn't ask my parents any questions. I didn't want to know the answers. Thinking that dawn could not be far away, I rose and put on a dress and apron. I moved into the next room and stoked a fire, watching it with heavy eyelids.

The sound of footsteps made me turn to see my mother. Her nightgown trailed on the floor as she walked over to me, her long, ebony braids glinting in the firelight. "Can't sleep?" she asked gently.

I shook my head.

Sitting down next to me, she put an arm about my shoulders, and I couldn't stop the tears.

"Oh, my Bethy." she whispered, planting a warm kiss on the top of my head. "Will you ever know how much you mean to me?"

Thunder rolled in the distance. I wiped my face clean on my apron, and set my head on my mother's shoulder. The thunder grew louder. "What is that?"

My mother held a finger to her lips.

The curtain slid open, and my father stepped out with a lantern in his hand. The sound stopped quite abruptly, and he looked at my mother. "Horsemen."

Mother's eyes widened. He was right. That was not the sound of thunder, but of horses riding at a full gallop. But why here, at this time of night? We both stood, and she took me by the hand, leading me to the curtain. "Elizabeth, stay here." Her voice was tense, her lips tight, and her eyes wide. She stepped through the curtain and drew it closed behind her. A sharp rap on the door made my heart pound. I heard my father open it.

"Is this the home of Master John Atlee?" The words were short and concise.

"It is." my father answered slowly.

"Search the dwelling."

Hearing the command, I crept toward the curtain and peeked through a hole. Several soldiers had entered the house, and had begun to search the front room.

"We have nothing of value if that is what you seek." My father carefully chose his words.

"We shall see." I caught a glimpse of the man, who was giving out the commands. He was thin, and his face was twisted into a sideways smile. His eyes darted about the room as if always searching for something. My hand went to my pocket where the gold necklace lay tucked in between the pages of Peter's letter. I hadn't told my parents about either the pendant or the letter. Now, I regretted it. What if that's what they were searching for?

"Have you any acquaintance with a young man by the name of Peter Lockton?" the commander asked.

"I do." my father answered.

"And did he take up residency here?"

"He did."

I watched my mother's eyes flit from the commander to my father as if she were waiting for one of them to explode into a rage.

The commander's eyes swept the room and landed on the curtain I was peering through. I backed away from the curtain. I could not tell if he had seen me, but the sideways smile had seemed to deepen on his features. It occurred to me to run out the back door leading to the yard and find a place to hide until this was all sorted out. I turned to do so, but the door was already open, and another soldier had just stepped through it. He was broad shouldered, and I could not even guess at his towering height. Neither could I see his face under the hood of his cloak. I stepped backward with a scream stuck fast in my throat until I backed into the table. He advanced a few steps toward me, and my hand touched what I knew to be a kitchen knife behind me on the table.

"Miss Atlee, I have orders to escort you away from here." came the deep voice.

"To where?" My fingers gripped the handle of the blade.

A sharp crash from the next room caught my attention. He seemed to take this opportunity and sprang from his place, catching hold of my wrist. I screamed in pain, and with no preconceived plan, struck with my knife. It must have had the desired effect, for he reeled back clutching his right forearm. Astounded at my own handiwork, I gasped, letting my weapon clatter to the ground. Suddenly, the room flooded with light as the curtain was drawn back. I turned to see the commander, standing in the doorway of the room. For a moment, all was still. I took it all in; the despair on my mother's face, the commander's sunken smile, and the defeat of my father's expression. His eyes traveled from me to the hooded soldier next to me, and for the briefest of moments, a hopeful smile brushed my father's face. He looked down at the lantern in his hand then to the doorway. With all his might, he threw it out the open door. It landed with an audible shattering sound. Through the window, I saw flames licking up the dry grass. All turned to see the fire. Soldiers poured out the front door trying to save and catch their frightened horses, yet Father never moved. His eyes narrowed, and giving me a confident nod he mouthed the word, "Go."

He is giving me a chance to escape. But the thought came too late. The tall soldier behind me gripped my arm, dragging me toward the back door.

"No!" I shrieked, fighting to grasp something, anything. I caught hold of the doorpost and gripped for a few moments before my fingers gave way. I did not cease my screaming. My calls for help, however, went unanswered. My captor caught hold of one of the loosed horses and pushed me onto it, mounting behind me. At his kick, the animal surged forward, and we dashed around the house to the path. I caught a glimpse of our home, now ablaze. My mother saw me through the window. Involuntarily, I lurched in the direction of the house, but a strong arm came down like a bar between me and the ground rushing past. The soldier behind me urged the horse onward, and my home grew smaller and smaller in the distance until the trees hid it from view. The tears stung my eyes, and it was all I could do to grasp the horse's mane. As we dashed down the road, I looked through bleary, tear-filled eyes for the lights of the village, but no lights came into view. We rode for some time, our speed in no way decreasing, but the town never appeared. All of a sudden it occurred to me. We weren't going toward the town. We were heading in the opposite direction. I suppose I had still held some hope of being able to escape once we reached the village, but we were only riding farther away.

Trying to devise a plan, I looked to my right. A thick line of trees rushed by bordering that side, and a field rolled along the other. We began to ascend a hill, slowing as we did so. I would have to be fast. Horrible images began to play in my mind. What if I only jumped halfway off, before he caught hold of me, and I ended up being drug along behind him? The horse stumbled, and I saw my chance. For a brief moment, his right hand dropped the reins, and I leapt from the horse's back. A hand caught hold of my shoulder as I swept through the air, but he couldn't hold on, and I hit the ground. I had expected an easier landing, but as my hands and knees connected with the road, it seemed to fall away under me. I felt myself rolling down the hill gaining speed when with a sharp Crack! I came to a stop, staring up at the sky. I tried to get a breath in, but it wouldn't come. I realized the crack had been my head striking against something. As I looked to the top of the hill, I saw the rider, black against stars, turn the horse and begin to charge back down the hill. Unsure if I could even move, I tried to stand, and with a stumbling stagger, headed for the forest.

I groped in the darkness, trying to find a place to hide. I could hear him crashing through the trees behind me, and though my head throbbed, my feet pressed on. My right hand brushed against a tree trunk. It was the best place to hide, for now. I ducked behind it, hoping that my pursuer's vision in the dark was as inept as mine. As I crouched in the shadows, I listened. No sound of someone crashing through the brush. No sound at all. Smiling to myself, I wondered how far he had followed me before giving up. A massive hand suddenly closed over my mouth. I fought and struggled, but his grip was firm. How had I not heard him behind me? I soon found that my shrieks and efforts to escape were useless.

"Be still." he whispered. "I mean you no harm."

Reaching up, I tried to pry his fingers off of my mouth. It was then that I felt the scars on the back of his hand. No, not scars, burns. His hands were rough and wrinkled, as though they had once been badly burned.

Chapter 6

"Isaac Colt!" I screeched.

His hand was instantly back over my mouth. "Quiet!"

"What do you think you're doing?" I hissed as he removed it again.

"I was trying," he gasped between breaths, "To save you from being caught and killed, but you are making it rather difficult."

"You could have let me recognize you!"

"I thought you did." he insisted.

"Well, I didn't."

"Yes." he laughed. "I noticed, just after you stabbed at me with a kitchen knife."

My ears began to ring as tears formed in my eyes. "I—I didn't know. I thought…" Sobs destroyed any resolve I had to finish.

"I know." he replied in a tone that reminded me of my father. "I *am* sorry. I never meant to get mixed up in all of this. I'm only trying to keep a promise to a friend." A chuckle crept into his voice. "I just never dreamed it would be so difficult." He stood to his feet. "Are you alright?"

I nodded. Honestly, I was cold, terrified, and pain was pounding through my head, but under the circumstances it didn't seem worth mentioning. Grabbing hold of the tree, I pulled myself up, but the smooth papery bark nearly made me slip. I caught hold of a low branch as a dark haze began to blur my vision. A rushing sound filled my ears. I felt a strong hand on my shoulder, and looked up to see Isaac standing next to me. He was saying something, but his words were lost to me. My head was light, and I couldn't think clearly. The darkness closed in around me, and I fell forward.

—ɯ—

I could feel a hand on the back of my head, pressing the place that was bleeding. I felt myself being carried as icy needles dug into my skin, through my clothes. I couldn't open my eyes for their stinging.

"Elizabeth!" I heard a voice call. I opened my eyes briefly and caught a glimpse of my own breath, misting in the air through rain, not needles. Ice-cold rain fell from a darkened sky. "Elizabeth, stay awake." The voice begged, panting hard.

I couldn't. Sleep reached for me as if trying to pull me backward off a cliff. I felt my position shift, and I found I could open my eyes now, without being blinded by the rain. I was being cradled, like an infant. On any other occasion, this would have embarrassed and annoyed me, but I was so tired, and it seemed much better than walking. I looked up to see the face of Isaac Colt, soaked with rain as his breath came in quick, oversized clouds. It did not make sense to me. Why was he here? I couldn't remember. I soon saw out of the corner of my eye, a horse. When we reached it, he set me on its back. I was warmer. I could not determine why for several moments, but as I regained my senses, I felt cloth surrounding me and I saw the dark green color of a familiar cloak. He mounted behind me and leaned forward, assuring that my hands were gripping the horse's mane.

"Hold on." The words were short and quiet, but I tried to obey them. He kicked hard, and he urged the horse forward with a shout.

I found myself drifting away, no matter how hard I tried to hold on. My eyes would close, and I would begin to lose consciousness when a jolt would awaken me. He guided the horse off the path, dodging trees, and low hanging branches. As we came to a stop, I saw a house hidden in the forest.

"God, please!" I heard him whisper behind me. "Alice!" he called. "Alice Fitton, are you at home?"

A lamp was lit in the house. A woman came out, followed by several other people. "Isaac? What on earth?"

"Alice, just take her." he commanded.

I felt myself being lowered down from the horse, and I began to loosen my frozen fingers from the horse's mane. When next I opened my eyes, several faces were above me, lit by a dim lamplight. Everything seemed to be in motion. I spotted Isaac in the doorway, blood staining his right arm. Someone was speaking to him, but his eyes were fixed on me. I reached my hand in his direction, silently begging him not to leave me here. He held my gaze. Yet, even as he looked at me, he nodded to the speaker, and began to follow them out of the room. The door closed behind them, and I looked up at the faces. They seemed to close in all around me, and as they did, the familiar black haze began to appear. No. With what little strength I had, I pulled away from them, but hands restrained me, voices shouted, faces blurred, and all was dark.

——

"Do you see it?"

"Oh yes, can't you?"

"No mistake."

I sucked in a breath and coughed on the smoky taste of the air. Light burned my eyes as I tried to open them. I blinked and found myself lying on my side, staring into firelight. Had I fallen asleep in front of the fire?

"She's just a child." an unfamiliar voice whispered behind me.

I rolled over to see two figures, in the soft light, and felt panic rise in my chest. This was not my home.

A woman, the one who had spoken, saw me and drew her hand to her mouth. "Oh, Isaac."

I stared back at her, wondering if I were somehow injured or disfigured in a way that would make her react that way. My head pounded, and I found it difficult to breathe for the pain.

"Elizabeth." a deep voice echoed from the shadows. I turned to look as the voice's owner stepped into the light. "Do you know where you are?"

I shook my head, and as I did, pain shot through it. I pressed my hand to my head and felt cloth tied around it. I looked up at the face of the man who had just spoken, and as I did, a rush of images, memories, and pictures began to crash down on me. I closed my eyes but could not stop them. They flooded my mind. I heard the thunder, felt the hand on my wrist, and saw the kitchen knife clatter to the ground. I looked again into my father's narrowed eyes. He nodded. "Go." Trees rushing on either side, a rider, black against the stars, and rain falling, soaking through my clothes, and dripping from that same face which I now saw in the fire's glow. My face was wet with tears. I looked at Isaac and nodded. "I remember."

"Just what do you remember?" he asked as I sat up.

"I remember the house catching fire, and ..." A short gasp left my mouth. I gave each of them a pleading look. "If they're dead, please tell me."

"Well," The woman looked steadily at me as I braced myself for the worst. "The soldiers are still looking for them, which leads us to believe that they are both safe and are in hiding somewhere."

"I need to find them." I stood, yet as I did, the room began to spin and I sat again. As I caught my breath, I felt a light hand on my shoulder.

"You need time to heal, Dear." Her words were not comforting as intended. So, I was trapped here, wherever *here* was?

"Besides," Isaac cut in. "Your father and mother were not the only ones who disappeared that night. The guards are no doubt, searching for you as well."

"I have to find them. They need to know I'm safe."

"If that is to remain a reality, you must stay here."

"How long has it been?" I asked, looking to the tiny lady in front of me.

"You were brought here yesterday evening, just a few hours before dawn."

"Elizabeth." I looked up at Isaac. His face was earnest. "I promise you that we will do all that we can to help you find your parents."

I nodded, unable to speak.

"Well," The woman straightened to her full height, which wasn't much to speak of. "I suppose, I ought to find you something to eat."

Isaac stood also and stepped outside into what looked to be predawn light, closing the door behind him.

I looked up at the little figure still bustling about the semi-darkened room. What an odd character she seemed. Her features looked even smaller when completed by her dark eyes. As she reached for something on a shelf too high for her, I felt the impulse to get up and help her, but stopped myself. I was not yet ready to stand up and find the room swirling again. "I don't feel as if I could eat anything." I said slowly.

She clicked her tongue. "One must not live life through feelings, especially at your age." She gave me a sideways glance. "Believe me, I tried."

I stared at my surroundings. The room seemed too large for someone like her. The table could have easily seated more than ten people. On the mantle, behind me was the only piece of decor to be seen. A gold ornament in the shape of a leaf hung above the fire place. It looked very much like the one Peter had given me.

"Who are you?" I asked as I turned back to the woman.

Clambering down from the chair she had used to reach the object on the shelf, she sent a warm smile in my direction. "I suppose we never were properly introduced."

I shook my head.

"I'm Alice Fitton." She sat down near me, and began to unwrap the cloth to reveal a loaf of bread.

"I cannot pay you." I shoved it back in her direction.

She raised one eyebrow. "Who asked you to?"

I looked down and believed that meant I could eat some, but just as I brought a piece of it to my mouth, Alice bowed her head.

"Dear Father in Heaven, we praise You for all You have done. We thank You for Your mercy in sparing Elizabeth's life, and pray that Your Will may be done in finding her parents. We love You, and ask that you would bless this meal, in the Name of Jesus. Amen."

I stared at her for a few moments, yet she tore into her half of the bread, and only smiled.

"Where are we, exactly?"

She waited a moment, deciding what to say. Finally, she nodded. "Several miles north of Tonbridge."

"Why am I here?"

She smiled fondly. "I'm an herbalist, a sort of, physician, you might say, and Isaac knows I'll keep you safe."

"If I'm found here, what will they do to you?"

Her calloused hand, gripped mine with surprising force. "Allow me to be clear, Miss Atlee. I am honored to have you in my home." She seemed to be staring through me. "I never believed it was possible." she murmured in amazement.

Before I could question her, she rose and wrapped the remaining bread in cloth. I watched her face in the early light of day seeping through the window. Perhaps it was the light or the curious mist in her eyes, but her face looked oddly familiar. It was the faint memory of ... But she turned away, and I lost all hints. Still, something about her smile was so like someone I knew, but who?

She glanced back at me. "We need to find you something besides that old dress."

I glanced down and saw my filthy, tattered apparel. She walked over to a chest and lifted out a faded, but clean garment. As she handed it to me, her gaze seemed far away, as though she were looking through me to someone else. "This ought to fit you."

It did, perfectly. As I slipped it over my head, I remembered Peter's gift, and his letter were in the pocket of my dress. I picked it up, and reached into the pocket to find the pages, some of them still wet. The necklace, however, was gone. I tried desperately not to be upset. I had lost much more than a necklace in the last several days, but I had promised Peter I would protect it.

"Where did you get this dress?" I asked, stepping back into the dining room.

She didn't answer but stared out the window. "It looks like a lovely sunrise."

Catching a glimpse of the pink sky, I had a sudden urge to feel the chilled air on my face. Questions could wait. My head still throbbed as I pushed the door open and stepped outside. The world was fresh from the rain, and the little house in the woods was a transformed place from the one I had seen two nights before. The black bruise against the trees was one of the many images clouding my mind. Now, all of it was bathed in a pink glow as the sun painted the eastern sky. I sat down on the front step trying but failing to think clearly.

Footsteps crunched along the gravel, and I looked up to see Master Colt leading a horse around the yard. He smiled, motioning to the sky. "It's beautiful, is it not?"

I nodded and strained to see the mare better. "Is that the same horse?" True, my perception had been limited the other night, but I had remembered a black, unshakable animal, not the brown, bony nag he led around the yard.

"No." He patted the mare's neck. "This is Annie. I had to let the other go. I didn't wish to add horse thievery to our other crimes."

His word stuck fast in an unintended target, and ice frosted over my tone. "I truly am sorry, but if you knew it would be such trouble, why did risk your safety for a stranger?"

"I think we've had this discussion." he replied with force. "I had a promise to keep." He came a few steps closer and sighed.

I swallowed the tears, but could not keep my voice from shaking. "I just don't understand. No oath was worth all of this." I could not keep my eyes from travelling to the bandage on his arm.

He laughed. "You would be surprised. I do not make my promises lightly."

"You and Peter must be very good friends."

"Why do you say that?"

I shrugged. "Well, to make such a promise."

He studied the ground intently. "Peter is a friend unlike any other, but I must be honest. It was not him that I promised." He looked up at me. "It was your father."

I stared in astonishment.

His eyes lit, remembering something, and he reached into one of the saddle bags. "You dropped this." He held forth the gold shimmering necklace.

"Thank you." I said, taking it from him.

"That pendant meant a great deal to Peter."

"I know." I said, placing it in my pocket with the letter once again.

He turned to lead the horse back to its stall, but as my fingers brushed against the letter, I remembered something.

"Master Colt."

He looked over his shoulder at me.

"Peter gave me a message for you." I scrunched my eyes shut, trying to think of the words Peter had written in his letter. *Tell Colt* … "I don't know what this means, but he wanted you to know, that I have something you need."

He seemed as puzzled over the message as I was. "Do you happen to know what he was talking about?"

I shook my head. "I was hoping you would have some idea."

"I do." He nodded. "I just hope I'm wrong."

Chapter 7

"Are you sure that's what he said?" Alice asked, sitting across from me.

"Yes." I replied, not feeling perfectly truthful. He hadn't exactly said it, but what was the difference if he had written it?

"Did he give any inclination of what he meant?" Isaac asked me for the third time in the last two days. He had come to visit Alice, and they had talked for some time before approaching me.

"No." The letter in my pocket felt heavy. Perhaps it wouldn't have been wrong for me to show them, but what if they took the letter, and I didn't get it back? I couldn't do it. It was all I had left. "So what do you think he meant?" I asked.

They looked at each other. "I think he wants you to take his place." Isaac said cautiously.

"Take his place?"

"Child." Alice seemed to weigh her words. "Did Peter tell you what he does?"

"Only a little bit. I knew he was involved…" I bit my tongue, unsure of how much to say.

"In the translation of the Scriptures." she finished.

"We are also part of that work." Isaac said.

"Peter was working on a translation of the Psalms. When we arrived here, he had nearly finished them."

"He wrote the truth." I said thoughtfully. It made sense now.

"Yes." Alice went on. "Isaac has a brilliant mind for translating from the Latin, but…" She hesitated. "He can't write."

"Together, we planned to finish the Psalms, but plans changed." Isaac added as he folded his hands in front of him, and I realized he must have lost all feeling in them, when they were burned. "We've been praying for another writer."

I froze. They couldn't be serious. "Me? You think I'm the writer you've been praying for?"

"No." Isaac said, getting a sharp look from Alice. "But, apparently Peter did."

"Why would ask me to write for you?"

Alice sighed. "Peter wouldn't say something like that unless he was sure. It's given us something to think and pray about."

Isaac leaned forward, resting his elbows on the table. "You don't have to do this, and if you decide not to, we'll still help you find your parents, but we thought that perhaps you would like to make the decision for yourself."

"Thank you." I looked from one to the other.

Secretly, I was flattered. I knew this was a difficult job, and

Peter had still thought I could do it. I had never known he had such confidence in me. I promised them that I would think about it, and I weighed the decision for several days. What would my mother and father have said? They had never been exactly opposed to Peter's writing, but they hadn't ever encouraged it either. I knew my uncle would find it appalling, and I enjoyed that thought.

I had been thinking about it for days, when I finally came to Alice, and told her that I would do it. It wasn't just the excitement of it that helped my decision. Peter told me to keep searching for the truth, and here was the opportunity to not only search for it, but to write it. Alice was delighted when I told her, and said she would go into town the next morning to purchase ink and paper. So, the next morning I was left at the house, alone. I felt I had made the right decision, despite the whispering doubts in my mind. Isaac and Alice would still search for my parents, and if they were found soon, surely I wouldn't be obligated to finish. With these thoughts swirling around in my mind, I went into the extra room of Alice's home. It, unlike the others, had a door leading to it, a door which was usually locked. I realized it must have been Peter's study. Today, the door opened easily. It was simple, with only a desk, a fire place, and a window. I ran my hand over the desk's surface where a blank sheet of paper and a pen lay. I sat down, in the chair and thought of what it would be like to write here. In that moment, I was filled with a desire to write. It was like the music, but stronger. I picked up the quill pen and twisted it in my fingers.

A shriek sounded outside. Creeping to the window, I peered outside. A rider streaked down the hill on a white horse. I could just see him between the trees. All of the animal's muscles tensed as he recklessly turned off the road. With a shout, he guided the beast into Alice's yard and dismounted. I hurried to the door unsure whether to bolt it or to throw it open. Alice had said not to let anyone in. His feet thundered up the steps. I bolted it and waited for a volley of pounding and shouting. It didn't come. He tried the handle once. Finding it locked, he grew silent. I could still hear his heavy breathing on the other side, and dared to peek out the window. The man hurled something, shattering the window. I dove out of the way, to keep from being cut. Whatever he had thrown was now lying on the floor, covered in splinters of glass.

"I have a message for Alice." he said between breaths. "He's gone. He gave that to me, right before they took him. Eastbourne, at the cleric's house." His footsteps sounded on the porch, and he was gone. Standing, I stared out the window, through bits of broken glass. He swung himself onto the horse and steered the animal toward the road. I knelt to the floor, and brushed away the slivers that were covering what looked like a satchel; A distinctly familiar leather satchel. It was Peter's.

Shouting made me turn back to the window. The messenger had just reached the road, when two soldiers rode over the crest of the hill. He urged his horse onward, but the soldiers' animals were fresher and faster. One strung a bow and released it. It must have missed the man by a finger's breadth. Another arrow flew from the soldier's bow. A sharp cry sounded. The messenger fell to the ground. The shaft had found its mark. The soldiers, dismounted, and caught hold of the messenger's horse. The white, terrified beast pranced about its rider as the soldiers tried to hold it still and check the saddle bags.

With a gasp, I realized that what they were searching for was in my hands; Peter's satchel. I turned, pressing my back to the door and gripping the leather satchel with all my might. I could hear the hoof beats in the distance, and I knew that they were gone. I didn't move. I didn't breathe. What was I to do? Without thinking, I reached for the bolt. Closing my fingers around it, I drew it back and opened the door. The soldiers had gone, but there could be others. Somehow, I didn't care. I ran for the road where a still, moaning figure lay.

"Please!" he gasped. "There is not much time."

I knelt by him, shuddering at the sight of the arrow. He lay on his front, his face turned away, and though I tried to roll him over, he would not be moved for the pain. His hand seemed to be grasping for something, so I held it in my own, trying in some small way to ease his suffering.

"Just this;" His breath was growing more ragged with every second. "I have a daughter. I want her to know that I love her."

"What is her name?"

He didn't answer. His breathing stopped, and the warmth drained from his hand.

"No!" I rolled the body over and saw the face. It was Lord Garret.

Sybil. I said her name over and over. What would she do now, without a mother or a father? My heart twisted. I lifted my head to where the riders had disappeared down the road.

"He was a good man!" I cried. "And a good father."

"Elizabeth?"

I turned to see both Isaac and Alice standing a few steps away.

"There was nothing I could do!" I cried. "I tried to help, but, I was too late. Someone needs to tell Sybil." I began sobbing too hard to put words together.

Isaac nodded and walked toward the body.

"Come along, dear." Alice pulled at my hand.

I choked back a sob as she guided me back to the house.

"Start at the beginning." she whispered. "What happened?"

Trying to clear my head, I remembered why he had come. I ran for the house, without a word. Entering the darkened room, I found the satchel, still unharmed on the table.

Alice plodded up the steps. "Child, what do you think you're doing?" She stopped, seeing the shattered window and the satchel in my hand. "Lord, have mercy." she breathed. "Where did you get that?"

"It's Peter's." I held it forward.

"I know." She took it in her hands and lifted the flap. "Why do you have it?"

"Lord Garret," I started. "He said…" I closed my eyes, trying to recall the words. "He said he got it just before they took Peter in Eastbourne, at a cleric's house."

Alice seated herself in a chair by the fire, her fingers entwined around the satchel. I gazed out the window to see Isaac tying the body of Lord Garret to his saddle. I looked back, trying to forget the horrid sight, when I noticed Alice staring into the fire with tears in her eyes. I crossed the room and knelt in front of her.

"I should not have left you here." Her voice trembled.

"There was nothing else to be done." I consoled.

"Peter was to meet Lord Garret in Eastbourne, and give him the Latin transcripts for us to translate."

"So, he was part of this too."

She nodded. "As was his wife before she died." She stared at the broken window. "What happened here?"

I relayed the whole afternoon's events. Alice listened quietly, only asking the occasional question. When I finished, she looked down at the satchel in her hand. "Thank God that you were not seen by any of the soldiers."

"Alice."

She turned her misty eyes upward.

"Why are you part of all of this?" I asked.

She sighed. "I'm Peter's grandmother."

My mouth dropped open. "You?"

"Yes, I raised him after his parents died. When he was in Oxford University, he met a professor named John Wycliffe."

At the sound of that name, my heart hammered.

"Have you heard of him?"

"Yes." I didn't mention the fact that I had heard he and his followers were the scourge of our generation. As my uncle was quite sure that God hated these people, he loved to talk about them. So, I was not lacking in an education on the "Lollards" as they were known.

"He and Peter became close friends." Alice continued. "It was Master Wycliffe who gave us the task of translating the Psalms."

The words weighed on me, but I had to speak them. True, I had already said I would write, but the cost had seemed vague and somewhat heroic. Now, the image of Lord Garret's murder would never leave my mind. If that was the cost of truth, I wanted no part of it. "Alice." I faltered. "I don't think I can do this."

Chapter 8

"You want me to take her?" The voice jolted me awake. Looking around I saw that it was still dark, and I sank back into my cot, listening.

"It's safer this way." Alice's voice replied in the next room. Light sifted through the curtain, with shadows crossing in front of it from time to time.

"Eastbourne?" Isaac's voice echoed. "I can't take her there! What if someone recognizes her?"

"No one will."

"What if she tells someone?"

"She wouldn't do that." Alice disagreed.

"Well, perhaps not over afternoon tea." he grumbled. "But the authorities have other methods."

"Isaac." Alice chided in a low tone. "I can't take her with me to find Sybil. It's too dangerous."

"Alright, I'll take her." he sighed. "It's just that she's a child, the greater her knowledge, the greater the chance of her being harmed."

I resented his calling me a child. What was so awful about taking me to Eastbourne? I heard footsteps approaching and knew that I should be found asleep. I closed my eyes, and waited for Alice to wake me. The curtain slid open. She nudged my shoulder and whispered that it was time to get up. I nodded and rubbed the sleep from my eyes.

—⟶

As the sun peaked over the mountains, Isaac secured Annie to a cart, and Alice packed us something to eat. Alice was headed for London, to get to Sybil before anyone else did. Isaac was going to the port town of Eastbourne to see what he could find out about Peter. While I wanted to go with Alice, she insisted that I would be much safer going south with Isaac. When all was ready, Alice, took both my hands in hers and looked up at me. "Oh Child, how I shall miss you!"

I searched for words as I looked at this woman who had broken every assumption I had made about her. "Alice, I have never known anyone quite like you before."

Her fingers brushed my cheek, her face shined, reminding me of Peter. "We are not so remarkably different, you and I."

"I hope to see you again."

She nodded. "You shall. Safe journey." Her face crinkled into a smile as she embraced me one last time.

I climbed into the cart. As we bumped away, she stood, watching us. She was such a tiny woman, yet there was so much to this lady named Alice Fitton.

As I had never traveled much farther than from our home to the village, I was not accustomed to riding in a horse drawn cart. After several bumpy dust-covered miles, I was hoping I never would again. Not far along the road we met several armed men. They were not soldiers, but certainly not a group one wished to cross. They greeted Isaac but did not slow their pace. When they had passed, Isaac turned back to me. "Those men are Alice's escort to London."

I was suddenly much happier that I was not going to London.

"I understand that you spoke with Alice last night." he said.

I nodded. "I'm sorry I can't help you."

"As I said before, it was for Peter's sake that we considered it. I could hardly believe he would send a message like that."

A bit of the resentment I'd felt this morning sparked inside me. "Why not?"

He shrugged. "Well, it's a dangerous job, and a difficult one. I'm surprised he thought you were ready."

"Maybe he had more confidence in me than you would like to believe." I shot back.

"It's nothing against your ability." he defended. "But this is not an easy life."

I understood what he was trying to say, but still disliked his point. I could have done it. I just didn't want to.

As we rolled down the road, the early autumn sun beat down unmercifully. To make matters worse, I had to wear a cloak over my head to conceal my face, should anyone be riding by. I was exhausted and irritable, having spent half the night wide awake and the other half trapped in nightmare after nightmare. Yesterday's events were too real in my mind. Again, I had watched a life taken. Again, I had been unable to stop it.

"How often did you speak with my father?" I asked.

He looked down, studying the reigns intently. "Many times." He straightened. "Nearly every day."

"Did he know of the danger Peter brought with him?"

Isaac tapped his fingers against the reins. "I'm not sure." He pointed toward a hill in the distance. "We're nearing Eastbourne."

When we reached the town, Isaac stopped the cart on the side of the road and tied the horse to a nearby tree. I slid from my spot and felt the tingling sensation as my feet touched the ground. He instructed me to keep my hood up, and I obeyed, reluctantly.

"I have to find a friend of mine." he said as we stepped into the busy clangor of the town. We were surrounded by people. A mother yanked her child's arm, pulling him along behind her. The child saw us and stared. An elderly man lay on the side of the street, begging. His gaze followed us as we walked. His stare held mine. I didn't realize I had stopped walking until Isaac reached for my hand, pulling me along behind him. "We have to keep moving." he shouted over the noise.

I pulled my hand away, frustrated that he didn't think I could walk behind him on my own.

He stopped and glanced in the door of a shop, pausing as he looked back to me, as if deciding. "Will you—"

"I won't go anywhere." I promised. I knew I shouldn't continue, but the words found their way out. "I appreciate everything you've done, but you are not my father."

He sighed, "Just stay here."

I stared through the darkly dusted window. I could see him talking with the blacksmith. How little did he trust me, anyway?

With a sharp yank, someone ripped me backward by my hair. I gasped and spinning around, saw two huge green eyes looking up at me. They were so large and bright, that the woman's face seemed thin, and papery in comparison. "You're not from here, are you?" she rasped. "You look familiar though." She stared at me a moment more. Then her face transformed from it sunken state of scrutiny to wide-eyed terror. "Margaret?"

I stared nervously and dared a glance in the blacksmith's shop. Isaac and his friend were no longer there. "Madam." I tried. "I believe you are mistaken."

"No!" she screeched, pounding her cane on the ground. "No, that's the face of Margaret if ever I laid eyes on it. Be gone! Haven't you done enough to curse us?"

"What?"

"For two generations we've lived in fear of the evil you brought on this town."

"I don't know what you're talking about!" I shouted over her forebodings. "I've never heard of any such person! Leave me be!"

She blinked inquisitively. "Not Margaret?"

"No!"

Even in my fear, I could not help but be repulsed by the way, her face twisted in thought. "You're her ghost then."

I took two steps back. With one more glance, I saw that the blacksmith's room was still vacant.

"We don't want any more to do with ghosts and curses! Gone with you!" she shrieked.

I turned and dashed up the street. Without slowing my pace, I checked behind me. She did not pursue, but glared after me to make sure that I was leaving. With a thud, I felt myself knock into someone. I stumbled, but caught myself before I fell. "I'm sorry!" I yelled, and tried to push past them, but they wouldn't have it. Firm hands gripped my arm.

"Are you alright?" asked a man's voice.

"Yes, I'm sorry. Please let me go. I need to—"

"Elizabeth?"

I cringed, wishing for all the world that I had not recognized that deep, clear voice. "Hello, Uncle." I looked up at him.

"Heaven be praised!" He leaned forward and hugged me. "What are you doing in Eastbourne?"

I was about to answer, when the woman called. "I would be careful who you socialize with, Father Jacob! This girl brings nothing but trouble." She spat on the ground, and hissed something

I couldn't understand, before turning, and hobbling away, leaning heavily on her walking stick.

"What have you done to upset the old woman?" he asked.

"I don't know." I shrugged. "I think I reminded her of someone she disliked.

"I wouldn't trust that." he advised. "She's mad, and everyone knows it, except her and her godson."

"I'm so glad I found you!" I cried. "Do you know where my mother and father—"

"Shhh!" he cut me off. "Don't speak of such things in public." He then resumed his classic smile, strolling down the street with me as he might with any parishioner. "Really, I'm just thrilled to see you."

I felt the fire start in me at his harsh rebuke. Yet, taking his hint, I tried to make small talk. "So, what are you doing here?"

"Oh, it's a lovely town this time of year." he oozed. "Delightful, really. I've come to see some friends off."

The word "friends" made my heart quicken. "Oh? Anyone I know?"

He gave a faint chuckle. "Oh no, just some old acquaintances of mine. They've been staying with me for the past week, and though I love guests I am glad to see them leave. It will be …" He scoured his brain for the perfect word. "Beneficial for them."

His meaning was not lost to me. "When do they go?" I asked, trying not to let the heat rise to my face.

"I've just come from the docks where their ship was anchored.

Normally, I would not have gone to such lengths, but I wanted to wish them safe travels."

I stopped in the street, unable to keep up the charade. "They're gone?"

He put a hand on my shoulder, ushering me down the street a bit faster around a crowd of vegetable carts. "They had no reason to stay."

"Have they no children?" I hissed between clenched teeth.

"A daughter and a son." he replied, without one slip in his pleasant attitude. "Sadly, their son died of the fever a year ago, and their daughter was kidnapped and killed."

I felt my knees give way. My uncle reached for me, to keep me from falling. "They think I'm dead?" I managed.

"This afternoon sun!" he exclaimed. "Just look at what it does to you. Ah, here we are." He led me up the walkway to a grand house, facing the water. As soon as the door closed behind us, he sat me down in a comfortable chair and settled himself in one just like it. "We got word yesterday. They said that the man who took you that night saw no reason to let you live."

"No." I protested. "I'm alright, really. Can you help me get to them?"

He smiled almost fondly. "Of course. It's just that…" A troubled expression crossed his face.

"What is it?"

"How did you get here?" he asked.

My throat felt dry. "Well," I peered through the lace curtains at the window. "He'll probably be looking for me." I said under my breath.

"Someone's looking for you?"

"No!" I argued. "Not like that. Friends of mine, from Tonbridge are helping me look for my parents."

"But you were all alone in town." His gaze searched mine, and I looked away.

"Just for a little while. They truly are helping me. They'll be worried. I should go." I stood and was almost to the door.

"Elizabeth."

My hand stopped just above the door latch.

"Do you really believe that these people are trying to find your parents for you?"

I turned around to face him, trying to keep my voice from shaking. "Of course they are."

"Elizabeth, you're a very sweet, trusting girl, but trust can be dangerous. If they really are searching for your parents, then why haven't you found them yet?"

"It's just taking them longer than they thought it would." I insisted.

"So, they are trying?"

"Yes…" My voice wavered.

He sat back in the overstuffed couch. "Well, that's fine, I suppose, if you want to search all over the country for them."

I hung my head. "Of course I don't."

"Well, then sit down and we'll talk."

I obeyed, surveying my uncle's parlor. Just like in the rectory, everything was immaculate.

He turned a compassionate look on me. "You miss them, don't you?"

Tears sprung to my eyes, and I nodded.

"It's alright." He set his hand on mine.

"I've been trying." I sniffed. "There's just no way to find them." I looked up to see him watching my face intently.

"I'll get you back to them." he promised. "Just tell me who's looking for you." His gaze was so honest.

"I can't. I promised."

"Elizabeth, what's more important? Your parents think you're dead. Think of your mother. She's lost two children already. She can't lose you too."

My lips trembled with the name. Just one name. That was all. One name and I would be saved from this nightmare.

Chapter 9

"Colt." My voice broke. "Isaac Colt is the one looking for me." I hunched forward, burying my face in my hands.

He patted my shoulder. "It's alright. I'll take care of everything." When my sobbing didn't stop, he tilted my chin upward. "Now, listen to me. You did the right thing. Any promise you made to him means nothing. Isaac Colt is a thief and a rebel who has never kept a promise in his life."

I sat up straight, my eyes wide. Horror overtook me. Never kept a promise? Except the one that saved my life. What had I done?

"No more tears." He grinned. "I'll make us a cup of tea."

I stared at the ironic set of china in front of me, feeling sick.

I could hear my uncle boiling water in the next room. "Your parents left on a ship to Dieppe, France this afternoon. I'm sure we'll find them within the next few days." he called. "Don't worry, that Colt fellow will be dealt with."

I stared at the ground, my heart pounding. *Dealt with.* What did that mean? Imprisonment, a trial, an execution? An image tore into my mind, unbidden. He could be murdered on the highway like Lord Garret. For what? Protecting me? Oh, I had made such a mess of this. Through the lace curtains, I saw Isaac across the street, searching for me. Words from Peter's letter flooded to my mind. *"Take courage, and be strong."* My gaze fell on the door latch.

By the time I was on the street, I couldn't see Isaac. I began to run, shoving my way through crowds of people. "Isaac!" My voice couldn't be heard over the throngs. I turned a corner into an alleyway and ran right into him.

He took hold of my shoulders. "Where have you been?"

"My uncle knows you're here." I said breathlessly.

His eyes widened. "You spoke with him?"

I nodded.

"We need to get out of here." He turned and started down the alley, then realized I wasn't following. "What are you doing?"

I searched for an answer. "You'll travel faster alone."

"What?" He stared at me, when panic spread over his face. "Look out!"

I turned, but too late. The soldier's knife cut into my upper arm as I twisted around. His hand was around my shoulders, wrenching me backward. "Isaac, go!"

He sped toward me, delivering a blow to the man's jaw. The soldier's grip loosened just enough, and I slipped away. Isaac caught my hand and pulled me down the alley. We turned down a number of side streets until I lost track. It was all I could do to keep up with him.

"We're almost there!" he called over his shoulder as we neared the city gates.

I pushed myself hard for several steps more but stumbled, landing in a cross section of the alleys, with buildings at each corner. Isaac hadn't noticed and kept running toward the city gates. To the street on my right, I could see the harbor. One ship was left, and ready to sail.

"Elizabeth!"

I shot a glance down the street on my left to see my uncle at the end of the alley.

"Do you really think he's going to help you?"

I stood to my feet, and watched Isaac turn at the city gates.

"Make your decision now." my uncle advised. "But know that I will hunt you down and find you wherever you are."

I turned my gaze on my uncle, and for the first time saw him for what he was. "Peter was right." I said. "You would do anything." Without looking back, I raced toward the gates.

My heart thrashed as I fled the city. When I reached the gate, I stopped. Isaac was gone. He had disappeared, and I was alone. Where could he have gone?

"Elizabeth." A voice whispered.

I glanced from side to side but saw no one.

"Here!" I turned to my right and saw two dark eyes just behind the branches. I slipped into the greenery, so relieved I could have cried. Isaac grinned and knelt in the bushes. "Get down." he whispered.

I crouched down on my hands and knees, still gasping for breath. He held a finger to his lips. My breathing was too loud, but what did he expect me to do? Withdrawing a handkerchief from his pocket, he offered it to me. I stared at it for a moment, when he motioned toward my shoulder. I glanced down to see the sleeve of my dress ripped, and bloody. I had felt a dull throbbing, but at the sight of my arm, the pain found its voice, and I wanted to scream. Taking the rag, I pressed it against my arm, and it stung. I bit my lip hard to keep from making noise. Footsteps thundered down the road. Neither of us moved. From his vantage point, Isaac had been able to see them. "Soldiers." he mouthed. The steps grew faint and disappeared. I sighed with relief, and leaned back to stretch out my tingling feet.

"Quiet." he whispered. He was listening to something. I leaned forward, trying to hear. Voices were coming closer. Through the trees, I could see the swords at their waists and hear the clinking of their metal armor.

"What went wrong?" one of them asked.

"Oh, he promised her everything. I was listening." the other replied. "He would protect her. He would get her back to her parents. She could have had anything she wanted."

"You mean he would have done that?" asked the younger voice.

"Of course not, Fool! Why do you think I was there? He's trying to kill her."

My mouth dropped open, and Isaac threw his hand over it.

"Father Jacob won't be satisfied until he has the matched set."

"So what is he going to do?"

"Threaten her, bribe her, kill her parents. How should I know? Just keep looking."

"They're probably half way to London by now." the younger voice complained.

The trees to my right rustled as one of them pushed it aside. Isaac removed his hand and looked at me. "Run!"

I stared at him blankly.

"Now!" he cried, shoving me to my feet. Right behind me the branches crashed down, revealing the two guards. My numb feet stumbled deeper into the woods. I heard the struggle behind me, but kept running. Pain shot through my feet with every step. The sound of my heart drummed in my ears. I could hear them drawing closer. I couldn't keep running. A cry split the air. Whose voice cried I couldn't tell. I stopped and listened. Silence. No one followed. No footsteps pounded behind me. All was still. A sound startled me. There, between the trees, stood one of the guards. His back was to me, but his head began to turn. I edged backward, reluctant to leave. What if the cry had been Isaac? His last instruction broke through my clouded thoughts. *Run.* I turned and sprinted up the hill, away from the soldier. He called after me, but I didn't listen. Why didn't he shoot? I burst through trees and found myself in a clearing. I was at the top of a hill, looking down on the city of Eastbourne, but hidden from the road. Just in front of me there lay a house. It was charred and had only half a roof. The walls still stood with cracking, blackened posts. It was terrifying, but something about the place stole my breath. Over the front door was hung a sign that read the word *"Maledictus"*. I recognized the word. My uncle said it often. It meant cursed. I pushed the door aside. If this place were cursed, perhaps it was where I belonged. The floor was white with ash. Suddenly, my knees could not hold me any longer, and I crumpled to the floor, sobbing. If Isaac was dead, it was my fault. If I was alone, it was my fault. If my uncle killed my parents, it was my fault. Oh, why had I gone to him? Why had I listened? Isaac was the only help I had, and I had sold him to his enemy.

—⁂—

I opened my eyes, staring into the flames. With a start, I backed away. It was just a fire pit, surrounded by stones, and the only light in the darkness. Where had it come from? I didn't even remember falling asleep, but I must have. A noise drew my attention to the doorway. Isaac stepped into the light. At seeing me, he smiled, and I burst into tears. He sat down on the other side of the fire.

"I thought you were dead." I said, trying to regain control.

He shook his head.

I stifled my sobs and brushed away the remaining tears. "What happened?"

"I tried to keep them from following you." he shrugged.

I waited for more of an explanation. He didn't offer one.

"I looked for you for so long." he said. "I never thought you would have found this place."

"What is this place?" I asked.

"The Old House of Curses." he replied, tossing another stick into the fire.

My eyes darted from side to side, expecting something to jump out at me from behind a piece of charred wood. "Where did it get that charming name?"

"The people who lived here died so unexpectedly that everyone in town blamed it on their sin."

A crash of thunder made me jump, and a little scream escaped me.

"It's just superstition. I actually knew the people that lived here."

"Really?"

He nodded. "He was a good man of simple trade, and she had a voice that would have charmed kings." He glanced around at the blackened remains of a home.

"When did it happen?"

He shrugged. "More than ten years ago."

"It hasn't been destroyed?"

"No one wanted to touch it. The people of Eastbourne have always been superstitious."

I gazed at several sparks floating in the ashes. "Isaac, did you live in Eastbourne?"

He gave a slow nod. "Most of my life."

"What happened?"

"Two years ago, my house went down in flames, very much like this one. My wife was killed in the fire." he answered. "I came too late to save her. We had a four year old daughter who was in the house as well. I found her trapped under a pile of burning rubble. We barely escaped with our lives."

"Then, she lived?" I asked.

He unconsciously rubbed his scarred hands together. "She did, but my wife's sister told me that I was incapable of raising her. I refused and resisted, but this woman was a wife and mother of five little ones. I thought I was doing the right thing by letting my daughter go. Not a day goes by that I don't regret that choice. The family lives north of London, as far as I know, but I've had no word or seen my daughter since."

I stared, wide eyed at him. "I didn't know."

"You have to trust me. I am trying to get you back to your parents. I know what it means to a father to lose his little girl."

His words silenced me. All this time he had treated me like a child. I had fought it. I had resented it. Now, I realized it was an honor that this man would treat me like his own daughter.

He stirred the fire and looked up at me. "Did Chancley really promise you all of those things?"

I nodded.

"Did you believe him?"

I nodded again. "My parents think I'm dead. He said he would get me back to them."

Isaac didn't ask any more questions, and I was thankful. I just couldn't tell him what I had done. "Did you know he was trying to kill me?" I asked.

"I'm not convinced that he was."

I stared at him. "How can you say that? You heard the same thing I did."

"I know that he was threatening to hurt you. I'm not sure that he would have."

"Why does he hate me?" I cried. "What have I done?"

"It's not about what you've done. It's about who you are."

"What does that mean?"

"It means you are powerful, that you could do great things. You are one of Chancley's biggest threats, and you don't know it."

"I don't understand."

He sighed. "As long as he can keep you thinking that you are worthless and helpless, he won't really hurt you."

"But I am!"

"Who told you that?" he challenged. "Did Peter ever say that to you? Did your parents raise you to believe that?"

"No."

"You see the fact is, Elizabeth, you could be a mighty messenger for God, and that scares Chancley to death."

"But I'm not mighty." I argued. "I'm not brave like you and Peter. I'm just…" I struggled searching for a word. "I'm just me."

"On your own." he agreed, softening his tone. "Not many mighty, not many noble, are chosen. The ones men would push aside, God chooses. You are helpless without Him, but with Him, you could change lives."

I stared at the ground. "God doesn't want my help with that. I just ruin things. That's the real reason my uncle hates me."

Isaac pushed himself to his feet. "I will not keep saying what you will not hear." He kicked dirt on the fire, smothering it. "Dawn is in several hours. Sleep while you can."

Chapter 10

In the dark I lay awake, attentive to every sound. My thoughts echoed as loudly as if I had shouted them. Several times tears slid down my cheeks, and I tried to keep my sobs quiet for fear of making too much noise.

Something outside cracked and rustled in bushes. I lay perfectly still, listening. Surely it was an animal. Yet, my heart still pounded. I rose from my place, and crept toward the doorway, peeking out. A dark form shadowed against the moonlit landscape. I didn't breathe. The man stood near the horse and cart, one hand on the horse's back, staring at the stars. His head turned, and I saw that it was Isaac. I sighed, and was about to lay down again when his voice caught my attention. "Please guide me." he whispered.

Afraid, he would hear me, I turned and tiptoed back to the corner I had occupied before. His prayer reminded me of a song Mother had sung to me years ago. It was a song her own mother had written when her father had been away, on one of his merchant trips.

When you are alone, my darling, when you are alone
If storms or troubles take you, lead you far from home,
I'll pray the angels light the sky, to shine upon the sea
And God Himself will guide you, and bring you back to me

The song made me smile, despite the ache in my heart. "I'm trying." I said in a hushed voice. "I'm trying to get back to you."

Footsteps sounded on the threshold. Isaac stood above me. "We need to go."

—⚡—

A chill crept under my cloak and crawled up and down my arms. We hurried along the back roads, sometimes using no roads at all. When we came across a stream we would stop to drink and rest, but only briefly. We had to keep moving. Despite the sun, we kept our cloaks draped over us to keep from being recognized. All day I agonized over how to tell Isaac I had betrayed him in Eastbourne. I couldn't. If I did, he would at the very least, despise me. I was weak. I had failed them. When the sun was directly above us, we had reached the woods surrounding Alice's home. Isaac said she was not expected to return until tonight, or tomorrow. We stopped at the well, some distance from the house, and drew the bucket up.

"Did you ever find out anything about Peter?" I asked, splashing some of the water on my face.

"I did." he said. "He was arrested in Eastbourne, and is being held in the prison there."

"Will they—That is, can they execute him?"

"Not on the suspicion of being a follower of Wycliffe, but if Chancley wants him dead, he could make up any number of accusations." Isaac's jaw tightened. "He's good at that."

There was an aching pit of my stomach. "Is there anything you can do?"

The breeze rustled the trees above us. He stared at the ground. "We're not an army."

At his words, my heart sank. "But there must be something." I said as he studied a low hanging leaf. "You must know someone who can help us. You can't just let him die."

"Do you think I want to?" he exploded. "Peter's the reason I'm still here. If he hadn't found me, who knows where I would be?" He crushed one of the leaves in his hand. "The last thing I want is to stand by while he dies for saving blind, stubborn people like me."

"Like us." I said more to myself than to Isaac.

He turned away.

I stepped toward him. "Then, what are you going to do?"

He stared, unseeing, at the horizon, when his eyes widened. "Finish the translation."

"What?"

"I mean it. We'll finish the Psalms."

"I don't understand."

A grin broke out on his face. "Why has Peter been arrested?"

"For being a translator?"

"That's what the priests and bishops would tell you, but ask any government official and they'd say that Peter Lockton is being charged as a seditious, and heretical rebel."

"Isaac, I don't—"

"Wait." He held up a hand. "You see, some of the Psalms are already legal. Several of them are printed in the prayer books and the breviaries, and if one Psalm is harmless and promoted by the church, why not all of them?"

"You're going to try and convince the clergy of this?"

"Not just the clergy; the governors, and the nobles, and anyone else who will listen. If what Peter wrote wasn't illegal, they can't hold him as a prisoner."

"And if it was, you would go to prison right along with him."

"It's worth the risk."

"Is it? Isaac, it's such a slight chance that anyone will even hear you."

"Someone will. Many of the nobility are against the Church's authority, just like Lord Garret was." he insisted.

"But the translation isn't even finished."

"You and I could finish it in a week."

"No."

The enthusiasm died on his face. "What?"

"No." I repeated. "Isaac, I want to help Peter just like you do, but I can't be a translator. I'm already further into all of this than I ever wanted to be."

"But it could save Peter's life."

"And I would just ruin your efforts! You know me. I ruin

things. I get myself into messes that I can't fix, and it puts other people in danger. I'm not going to do it again."

He stood perfectly straight, watching me. I didn't look away. I was serious. At last, he nodded. "I understand. I won't ask again." He turned toward the house, and I followed miserably behind.

As we trudged up the steps, I noticed that the door was ajar. It groaned on its hinges as Isaac pushed it a bit to reveal a darkened and abandoned room. Alice's neat little home had been torn apart. Furniture was broken into pieces and littered the floor. Every window was shattered.

"What happened?" My voice echoed off of the walls.

Isaac didn't answer. He shoved the remains of chairs aside, trying to get to the study. I followed him. We turned into the second room, which was also ravaged. Then I saw the door to the study. It was cracked in half. The wood was splintered, and dangling on the hinges. Isaac thrust it aside. Pages were scattered about the study. The only other destruction I could see was the cracked window just above the desk. Through the crevices, an eerie breeze whistled. It caught a page on the desk and blew it to my feet. Bending down, I picked it up and studied it; The familiar edge of the letters, the pleasant slant of the writing. This was Peter's work In fact, it was the translation.

"I don't understand." Isaac said. "Why didn't they take it?"

I crept forward. The wind brought an uncommon chill to the air. A knife pierced the desk, holding down a different parchment. Unlike those of the translation, the writing was dark and harsh as if scrawled in a hurry. I gripped the knife, but it would not come out. Leaning forward, I ripped the parchment out from under the knife and read. Tears blinded me, and my lips began to tremble. "Isaac, they weren't looking for the translation."

He looked up from gathering pages off the floor.

"They were looking for you." I held up the parchment, and he took it, studying every detail.

"It's a warrant." he said.

I nodded.

He looked back up in confusion. "A warrant for what?"

I stared down at the paper still trapped under the blade and saw the charges. "For kidnapping me." My voice shook.

He watched me, saying nothing.

I lowered into the chair by the desk. "It was me. I—I turned you in." The tears cascaded down my cheeks.

"I know."

"My uncle promised me those things so I would tell him, and I did. I told him that you were looking for me."

"I know."

"What?" I sniffed.

"I know you did."

"How?"

"Chancley's no fool. He doesn't promise without a purpose."

"But if you knew, why didn't you leave me in Eastbourne?"

"You made a mistake. I don't see that as a cause to abandon you."

"My mistake nearly killed you." I held his stare.

"God uses our mistakes."

I gazed at the cracked window pane.

"Yes, you stumbled. That does not mean you can't walk. God can take our failures and our mistakes and use them for His glory."

"How do you know?" I cried. "You never fail. You're the son of a bishop, a scholar, and a good man."

"Do you want to know what else I've been?" His voice rose. "I've been a terrible father, a blasphemer, and a drunk. When everything was taken from me, I found myself so turned around that I thought God was out to kill me. I thought He wanted to strike me down. I went to the Old House of Curses because I thought I belonged there. I had failed everyone, lost everything, and I thank God."

"Why?" I asked in astonishment.

"Because that's where Peter found me. God knew I was ready to listen. Elizabeth, we do fail, but God longs to pick us back up if we'll only let Him. If God could restore me, He could restore anyone."

I looked up at him. An odd haze had filled the room. It was smoke. I stood from my seat. Isaac saw it too. He moved to the doorway and shoved the door open. Flames burned in the other room. Covering his mouth with his sleeve, he motioned for me to follow him as he cleared a path. With one last glance behind me, I saw a bundle of pages and snatched it from the desk. I ran for the door. As I reached it, fire descended the doorpost and engulfed the doorway. It crumbled in moments, and I was trapped inside.

Chapter 11

I spun around, seeing the cracked window over the desk. I rushed to it, but before I reached it, it shattered from the outside. Climbing up on the desk, I saw a hand reach in, and I took it. The person on the other side gave a sharp pull, and I went tumbling out the window. The pages tucked under my arm flew in every direction. When I hit the ground, I lay there gasping. Whoever had pulled me out was now gathering up pages of the translation. I sat up, staring at him. He was wearing what looked like a hooded monk's robe. He shoved the pages into my arms, and took hold of my hand, pulling me to my feet. He led me up the hill, away from the fire, and when we were a safe distance away he turned my hand palm upward. In it, he set the gold chain and leaf pendant, which had slipped out of my pocket, and closed my fingers over it.

"Thank you." I said.

He nodded and then turned and ran toward the road. As he did, rain came sweeping up the rise, and he seemed to vanish into the mist.

Through the rain, I could see Isaac standing outside the building looking for me. I rushed back down the hill just as he was about to head into the blaze.

"Isaac!" I called.

He turned around to see me. "Elizabeth, what happened?"

"I'm alright!" I promised. "He pulled me out."

"Who?"

I stared at him blankly. "I don't know."

"Isaac Colt?" a voice called from behind us.

We turned to see several men on horseback, making their way through the woods. They stopped, and one of them dismounted. "We saw the fire. Is anyone inside?"

"No." Isaac said between breaths, trying to see the speaker better. "Nicholas?"

The man stepped forward and took Isaac's hand. "I had hoped to greet you under better circumstances."

"Why are you here?"

The rider motioned to the men on horseback behind him. "We've come all the way from Leicester to see you. We were riding to meet you on the road when we saw the fire."

"Well, I'm pleased to see you, but why all of you?"

"Master Wycliffe was determined to make the journey, to fetch the Psalms and few of us liked the idea of him traveling alone. Besides, there are things we must discuss as a group."

"Wycliffe is here?"

The man nodded. "He's staying at Garret Hall. We heard of Lord Garret's death when we arrived. His servants are fleeing, but have allowed us to stay there for the time being. We can take you back with us."

"We'd be grateful." Isaac shook the man's hand. It wasn't until his friend had gone back to the horses that Isaac sighed, and put a hand to his forehead. "The Psalms."

I looked down and realized I was still holding the translation under my cloak. "Isaac."

He looked down at me, and I held forth the pages in my hand.

"You got it?"

I nodded, smiling. "I got what I could."

He took it from me, shielding it from the rain.

"I hope it's enough for you to finish your work."

He examined the pages. "It's the Latin. I can still finish the translation." His face was hopeful again as he turned to me. "Thank you."

As I was about to mount the horse that was offered to me, I noticed the necklace, still in my hand. I slipped it over my head, watching the way it shimmered against my dark, filthy dress. Mounting the animal in front of me, I threaded the reins through my fingers and stared at the clouded sky. Maybe I didn't ruin things after all.

—⚊—

The one called Nicholas rapped on the door. Our horses shifted their weight. Through a series of twists and turns, the company had led us to Garret Hall. Instead of inquiring at the main door we were crouched at a servant's entrance. He knocked again. This time, the door opened a crack and we saw a face peering out into the darkness. The girl gasped when she saw us.

"Peace to you." Nicholas whispered.

"And to you." came the thick French accent as she opened the door wide.

We followed the girl down a darkened hallway. She held a candle out in front of her and moved noiselessly down the passage. She was clothed in black, no doubt mourning the loss of her Master, and she wore a dark cloak and hood over her dress. Never did she take her eyes off of the floor or turn to face us. Surely it was a habit after being a servant for so long. Several people rushed past us as we groped our way down the hall. After passing many doors, the girl halted and knocked on a specific one. Within moments, the door was opened by a short, paunchy man, whom I knew to be one of the Garret's servants. His eyes widened at seeing the men. "Come in." he said, stepping aside.

Isaac turned to me. "Stay here."

I nodded and sat down on the rough wooden bench against the wall. The door closed behind them, leaving the servant girl and myself in the hallway. Footsteps echoed down the hall as people passed. A mother carried a squalling infant in her arms. A frightened child with large hollow eyes followed closely behind a thin, work-worn man. All of them looked as though they were living in an eternal funeral service. No one spoke as they passed.

Even the youngest children didn't laugh, and giggle as children should.

"Where are they going?" I asked the girl.

"The Master has died. They have nowhere to go."

"Is Lord Garret's daughter not going to take over the estate?" I tried to catch her eye, with no success.

"She is young, and they fear that she would become a target."

"So, you're all leaving?"

She nodded.

"I'm so sorry." I looked about the hallway. "I used to come here often."

She nodded again.

"Mademoiselle!" a man called from down the hallway. "Nous partons."

"I come." she called back. "I must go." she said to me, but she made no motion to move. I waited for her to leave, but she only stood there.

"Can I help you?" I asked.

She said nothing, but stepped toward me until she was just above me. From a pocket, she pulled a piece of cloth and shoved it into my hand. She didn't move, or even speak, but waited for me to unwrap the cloth. I folded the corners back to see a necklace I remembered well. It was a small stone, which would have fit in the palm of my hand. In the center, there was an untidy hole, and through the hole, was laced a ribbon.

"Where did you get this?" I asked.

"It's yours." The French accent disappeared for the slightest of moments, revealing a familiar voice.

I looked up, but she was gone. She was wrong. It had once been mine until I had given it to...

"Sybil!" My voice echoed down the hall as I chased after her. I pushed past a group of people and reached the door. Throwing it open, I found myself in the starry darkness. A horse whinnied nearby, and I saw a carriage pulling up just in front of the house. The girl had just ascended the first step when I caught hold of her hand. "Sybil."

The green eyes that had once held such spark, looked down at me now dull, and full of tears. "I need to go." she whispered.

"He loves you." I gasped, breathlessly.

"What?"

"Your father—I was there, and he said that he loves you."

She stepped to the ground, eyeing me. "Do you mean that?"

I took both her hands in mine. "I give you my word, Sybil. They were his last words."

She burst into tears. "Oh, Elizabeth!" she sobbed, pressing her forehead into my shoulder. "I don't know why on earth they brought you here, but God sent you to me."

I was unable to find words.

She straightened, and wiped the tears from her face. "Why are you here?" Her eyes widened. "Are you going to write for them?"

"No, I..."

She waited for an answer.

"I'm here by accident." I managed

The wind stirred the branches above us. Sybil looked up at me. "Did you learn to write?"

I nodded.

"Then Bethy," She leaned forward. "This is no accident." She clasped my hand in hers. "You are the truest friend I have, Elizabeth Atlee."

We embraced one another, and she mounted the steps of the carriage. She closed the door, and the coachman shouted to the horses. As the coach rumbled away, she leaned out the window.

I lifted my hand, as I whispered, "Goodbye."

As I watched the carriage disappear down the drive, her words echoed in my thoughts. *"God sent you to me."*

"Elizabeth?"

I looked over my shoulder to see Alice just outside the doorway. I ran to her, and she threw her arms around me. "Oh Child, I was so worried."

I held her even tighter, trying to fight back tears.

Chapter 12

We slipped into the candlelit dining hall, unnoticed. Isaac and the other translators were gathered around a table in the center of the room. Alice led me to a table in the corner, where a bowl of soup had already been set out for me.

"Ridiculous!" said a spindly man sitting across from Isaac. "The authorities will not hear us. Besides you'll never finish in time."

"Are you saying that they plan to execute Peter?" aked a younger man in the corner.

"Chancley's name carries quite a bit of weight in the church." Isaac said. "If he gave the command, there would be few people to stop him."

"And yet you think we have time to translate the Psalms before he does?" the one across from Isaac challenged.

"It may be Peter's only hope." Isaac offered. "Please, you are six of the most influential men in the country. If the authorities will listen to anyone, it will be you."

"I doubt that." The comment came from Nicholas, who had been staring into the fireplace. "Repingdon, Aston, Bedeman, and I were recently excommunicated." he said, motioning to three of the other men in the room. "We've lost our teaching privileges at Oxford, and I'm afraid, our names won't do you much good."

Isaac sighed. "My friend, it's not your name I need, it is your help."

"Well I don't think it's wise to continue pushing the church." retorted the man across from Isaac. "They're serious about this. They mean to crush us."

An elderly looking man sitting in the shadows rose to his feet, and as he did, the room grew hushed. There was no doubt in my mind that indeed this was Master John Wycliffe. He turned to the spindly speaker. "Thank you, Master Repingdon." He then, turned his gaze on Isaac. "Master Colt, have you forgotten why we do this?"

"No, sir." he replied, looking down.

"Then why?"

"That men may know the truth."

The older man smiled, his eyes shining. "And the truth shall make them free. We cannot follow after the freedom of just one man. For if that man cannot be released, what then? Will we lose hope?"

"I understand."

"But perhaps, it is the will of God that this book be finished early. We came to collect the Psalms, for they are one of the last books needed to complete the translation. Let us finish the task before us, for we do not know how short our time is here."

Isaac looked up gratefully as the older man set a hand on his shoulder. "What we feel is temporary. What we do is eternal."

"Yes sir."

The room was quiet. No one argued. All of them listened with respect for this man. He looked around the room. "Who feels that God would have him stay to help this work?"

Four of the men stood in reply. To my surprise, one of them was the spindly man called Master Repingdon, who had argued with Isaac.

"These will stay." Master Wycliffe said. "Let us pray together, then the rest of us will be on our way at dawn." He lifted his eyes toward the heavens, and smiled. "We poor men pray Thee that Thou wilt send us shepherds of Thine own." the others joined in, speaking the long familiar prayer, some with bowed heads and closed eyes, others, staring upward, as if searching. "And Lord, give our king and his lords hearts to defend Thy true shepherds and Thy sheep from out of the wolves' mouths." I watched, wondering how these men could stand to be separate from their loved ones, how they could face prison and death for this work. Yet as they prayed a quiet strength seemed to fill the room. "And, Lord, give us, Thy poor sheep, patience and strength to suffer for Thy law." Perhaps I imagined it, but there seemed to be tears in the eyes of some. Master Repingdon, seemed to be locked in a battle with something unseen. "We ask this now, for more need was there never."

When the prayer was ended, the men began to file out of the room, but I waited. I turned to speak to Alice, but she too, had left. Only Master Wycliffe and Isaac remained in the fire lit hall, neither of them noticing my presence.

"One thing concerns me." said the older man, seating himself again. "You mentioned yourself as an active part of this work, and yet, if my memory serves me, you cannot write on your own. Since Peter's disappearance, have you found a new writer?"

I held my breath, now locked in my own unseen battle.

"No, but I trust God to send one." Isaac answered.

Sybil's words rang in my ears. *"God sent you."*

The conversation grew quiet as the men made their way toward the door. Seeing that I would soon lose my chance, I stood abruptly, the chair behind me scraping against the floor.

"Who's there?" Isaac called.

I stepped into the light, realizing that I must look like a spy. "I'm sorry. I didn't mean to startle you."

Isaac looked to his friend. "Master Wycliffe, this is Miss Elizabeth Atlee, Peter's student."

He gave a slight bow. "A pleasure to meet you, Miss Atlee. Next time you don't mean to startle someone, perhaps you should not sit so quietly in the dark." His eyes twinkled. It was not a rebuke. He began to walk toward the door again.

"Master Wycliffe." I started.

He turned and waited for me to speak, but my voice felt frozen. I swallowed, and took a deep breath. "I would write for Master Colt."

"Would you?" He eyed me, seriously.

"Yes." I said, staring at the ground.

"Why?"

I looked up, and met his gaze. "These people have done much for me. I owe them what little I can give."

"Is this the only reason?" he asked.

"No sir." I hesitated. "Peter Lockton said I ought to write for them."

He turned to Isaac, "Is that so?"

Isaac stared at me, dumbfounded. "It is."

Master Wycliffe studied me with keen eyes. "Do you understand just what it is you are offering to do?"

I nodded. "Yes sir."

"And do you understand the danger in which you are placing yourself?"

"I do." I said softly.

He leaned forward, placing a steady hand on my shoulder. "And have you made peace with God?"

Somehow I had known this conversation would lead here. "I believe in Him." I answered.

His expression became thoughtful. "There is so much more to God than simply believing in Him. Yet, something tells me, you already know that."

A gentle smile crossed my face. "Yes, I think I do."

"We are honored to have you join us, Miss Atlee." Even in his warm manner, there seemed to be a hint of astonishment in his tone.

"Thank you."

He turned to Isaac, who still seemed a bit stunned. "Well, I hope to see you both again soon. God be with you."

"And with you." Isaac said, as Master Wycliffe passed through the open doorway. He looked at me quizzically. "You didn't have to do that."

I thoughtfully brushed my fingers against the necklace. "I know."

—⁂—

Alice showed me where I would be staying. It was the first time I had ever had a room all to myself. It was nothing fancy, servant's quarters, in fact, but I felt like a queen.

The servants of Lord Garret were leaving to seek other jobs. Whole families were being uprooted, and Garret Hall would be left abandoned. Most of the servants had known about Lord Garret's involvement with the Lollards. Some were followers of Wycliffe themselves, which made this the perfect place to be a safe house, like Alice's. At least, that's how Alice had explained it.

After preparing for bed, I slipped beneath the covers, and lay staring at the ceiling. "I know we should have talked sooner. Perhaps if we had, I wouldn't have spent so much time wondering why I'm here." I took a deep breath, deciding to be completely honest. "I can't do this." I whispered in the darkness. "Not without You." I rolled over, gazing out the window on the moonlit landscape. "If You're there and if You don't hate me, I need to know."

The music came over me in a flood, but it was different this time. It wasn't a solitary world of my own. I knew I was not alone. He was the longing for truth, and The Someone I had been searching for. I pressed my eyes shut as two tears rolled down my face. He was there. He always had been.

—◊—

When I woke the next morning something was different. It took me some time to realize what it was. The indecision was gone. I no longer wondered whether this was right or wrong. Something in me knew that it was right. It didn't matter that my uncle would hate me all the more for doing this. What he thought, and even what he would try to do didn't matter because this was right.

The translating began that day. There were seven of us, altogether. The four men who had stayed to translate were all passionate about the work. Nicholas took the first section of the Psalms. Isaac and I took the second. Phillip Repingdon, the one who had stood against Isaac the night before, turned out to be one of the finest translators in the country. He had been excommunicated, and removed from Oxford, as had the other two translators, Lawrence Bedeman, and John Aston. They took the next three sections and we started to work.

I had forgotten how glorious it felt to hold a pen, and there was a new freedom about it that I had never enjoyed before.

When I wrote it felt as though it was what I had been meant to do. During the day, we would translate, and in the evenings, we would sit in the dining room, and one person would read what they had translated that day. They were wonderful, fire lit evenings. The seven of us, all huddled around a lamp on the table, listening to the Psalms.

The days flew by like this. All of the men finished their sections of the Scriptures and left them with us. When two weeks had passed, we were nearly done.

"*Gratiam et Gloriam.*" Isaac read.

I scrunched my face, trying to think. "*Gloriam* means... glory?"

"Yes." he replied. "And *gratiam?*"

"Means great?" I guessed.

"Grace." he corrected. "*Gratiam* means grace."

"Grace and Glory." I said aloud, before turning to write it down. Over the last few weeks, Isaac had given me a brief Latin education. My pen hesitated over the page.

"Is something wrong?" he asked.

"No, it's only that it sounds like something Peter used to say."

"Dei Gratia." Alice smiled.

"Yes." I nodded. "I always wondered what it meant."

"The grace of God." Isaac said quietly.

Alice lifted herself from her seat. "If you don't mind, Dear, I'm going to go get some rest."

"Of course." we answered in unison.

Her face crinkled into a smile, and she reached for the wall to steady herself as she walked.

We finished the next two Psalms within the hour. I looked over at Isaac. "Is that all of them?"

He was staring at the stack of parchment, but his face was troubled. "Yes."

I wanted to shriek for joy, but Isaac's concern halted me. "Is something wrong?"

"There should be more." he replied.

"More?"

"Yes, there aren't one-hundred and forty Psalms. There are One-hundred and fifty."

I leaned back in my chair. "They must have been lost in the fire."

Isaac sighed. "Well then, I suppose that one-hundred and forty will have to do. We need to start heading for Eastbourne. I had hoped to have the whole book finished."

A crash sounded from the other room, and both of us started to our feet.

"Alice?" Isaac called through the doorway.

There was no answer.

Chapter 13

Her face was hot. She was shaking and sweating. Her eyes were pinched shut as if in pain. Laying the quilts over her, we heard the struggling noise of her breathing.

Isaac knelt next to her and felt the burning forehead. "I don't know what to do." He stared at me hopelessly.

"Then let me." He stepped aside as I took his place. Staring at the fevered face, the realization struck me. "I don't either."

"What?"

"I don't know what to do." I panicked.

"Elizabeth!" he snapped. "Your father is a physician. Can you remember what he did for fevers?"

My mind cleared a bit. "We need a cloth."

We searched the room, but found nothing. "Take this." I ordered, ripping the hem of my dress.

He worked mechanically and brought the strip of material back, dripping with water from the pitcher in the next room.

I pressed it against Alice's forehead, and cheeks. Her head tossed away from the cloth, but I persisted.

"What does that do?" Isaac asked.

I stared at the faded fabric in my hand. "I don't know. I always saw my father do it. I assume it takes some of the heat."

Silence settled over us like storm clouds. She continued to thrash and moan occasionally.

"When does it start working?" he asked.

I studied her face, remembering the same flushed look on my little brother's. I couldn't lie to Isaac. "It doesn't always."

"Is there anything else we can do?" he pressed. "Did your father ever bleed patients when they were like this?"

"I don't remember."

I heard the soft tread of his shoes on the dirt floor. "Where are you going?"

He turned back to me. "We need help. Maybe there is a doctor in the town nearby."

"You can't bring anyone here."

"And I can't stand here and watch her die!" His answer made me jump as it echoed off of the wall.

"Isaac." Alice's whisper could hardly be heard, but she had our attention instantly. Her eyes opened. They were unnaturally bright. She stared at him earnestly, and her mouth moved, but it was impossible to hear her. She noticed our blank expressions and tried again. "Don't leave." The plea was not even enough to be a whisper, but it was understood.

"It will just be for a bit." he promised. "Elizabeth will be here with you."

She did not protest again, and he turned to leave.

"Isaac, wait." I called. "Maybe she's right. I won't know what to do if—"

"I need to go."

I glanced back down at Alice, and let my gaze travel upward again. "Please, hurry."

When Isaac was gone, I fetched Alice something to drink, but she couldn't swallow. I tried to stay calm, but my mind wandered, and I began to panic again.

"How long have you been ill?" I challenged her.

She tried desperately to clear her throat. "It rained."

"I don't understand."

She formed several words, but I could only make one out. "Sybil."

"You've been sick since you left to fetch Sybil?"

She nodded.

"That was weeks ago!"

She managed a weak smile. "Didn't want to be a burden."

"Alice." I fought back tears.

She reached over and touched my hand lightly. "Did you finish?"

My spirits rose. "Yes. It's finished."

She smiled. "Would you... Would you say it?"

I stood up. "I'll get it and read it to you, if you like."

"No!" Her eyes widened. "Don't leave. Tell me what you remember."

My mind spun, trying to recall a Psalm. I remembered one of the last ones which had need to be rewritten. With a deep breath, I closed my eyes. "I'll try." I waited until I could picture the page, the letters, the words. "Lord, I am searched and known. Thou hast known my sitting down and rising up." The words were difficult, and at times I forgot sections all together, but eventually, I reached the end. "Search me, and know my heart; try me, and know my anxious thoughts. See if the way of the idol is in me, and lead me in the way eternal." I broke into sobs and couldn't continue.

She gripped my hand in her own. "Child." She coughed. "Have you ever looked in a mirror?"

I stared at her, confused. "No."

"Peter… read a verse once. It said that this world is just a mirror… a mirror of Heaven." Her smile shone, but there was something in her eyes, that frightened me.

"Alice." I gripped her cold hand in mine. "Alice, please don't!"

She lay utterly still. Her eyes closed. There was no movement.

"Alice?"

She didn't answer.

"No!" Hot, angry tears spilled down my cheeks. Sobs wrenched my body.

"Elizabeth?" Isaac called from the doorway.

I couldn't answer. In moments, he was at her side, his face ashen.

"I—don't know what I did." I managed between sobs.

He bent over her and turned to me. "She's just asleep."

"Asleep?"

He nodded, reassuringly.

Fresh tears of relief filled my eyes, but I stifled them.

"Come in." Isaac called to someone in the doorway. Several people entered the room, all crowding around Alice.

"Who are they?" I asked defensively.

Isaac laid a hand on my shoulder. "Elizabeth, they're here to help."

"We need to move her." one of the men said.

"Why?" I cried.

The man looked me up and down critically. "It's too cold and damp. In this place, it's a wonder you don't all have the Black Death."

Together, they lifted her, carrying her limp body from the room.

I rushed into the hall behind them with an instinct to protect her rushing over me.

"Elizabeth!" Isaac caught hold of my arm.

"You can't just let them take her!"

"They know what they're doing. They can help."

"How do you know?" I shrieked.

He gripped my shoulders, looking me in the eye. "What is wrong with you? These people can save Alice's life."

I stepped back, stunned at myself. "I'm sorry." The entrance door slammed closed, the sound echoing down the empty passage. They were gone.

—⁓—

It was still dark when we mounted the horses. They had been Lord Garret's, and Sybil and I had ridden them many times. The satchel, carrying the translation, was slung over Isaac's shoulder. He promised me that Alice was in the best possible care, but whispers of doubt and worry crashed hard against my mind like relentless waves.

He turned to me. "Are you ready?"

I nodded.

He dug his heels into the horse's side, and I did the same. We raced down the moonlit road, the rhythmic pounding of hoof beats taking us still farther from Alice, yet carrying us closer and closer to Peter.

—⁓—

Eastbourne was in sight. We pushed the horses hard for this last leg of the journey.

"There's an abandoned chapel on the other side of the city." Isaac called over his shoulder. "It's where they agreed to meet us."

We skirted the edge of the town and dismounted the horses some distance from the chapel. Isaac had friends in Eastbourne, who had arranged a meeting with some of the nobles and other local authorities, who were sympathetic to our cause. The chapel itself had been abandoned years ago because the wood had begun to rot beyond repair. The steps creaked as we climbed them. Isaac pushed open the double doors, and the thick, moist smell inside nearly made me choke. The church was empty except for a rusting metal crucifix which hung on the wall opposite the doors.

"I can't have you in the meeting." Isaac said.

"Why not?"

"I don't want anyone to know that you wrote the translation."

"I don't understand."

He looked at me, his gaze solemn. "If this doesn't go as planned, I don't want you in danger of being arrested. I'll take the blame and the punishment for the translation."

We stood there in silence for some time. The pattern of the morning sunlight through the window moved across the floor as we waited. No one came.

"Where are they?" Isaac finally asked. Just as he said it, footsteps sounded outside. He looked at me, and pointed toward what had once been a closet. I hurried over, and tried to squeeze myself inside. Closing the door almost all the way, I peeked through the crack. The double doors opened, and light flooded the chapel.

"Repingdon." Isaac said, with obvious surprise. "Where is everyone?"

The door shut behind the tall, spindly man. "They're gone."

"Gone?"

He nodded.

"What happened?"

"The authorities have gone mad. I've never seen anything like it. They're blaming us for everything; the revolt, the people's unrest, Lord Garret's murder."

"But why?"

"I don't know. There was an execution yesterday. The rebels and murderers from Eastbourne's prison were put to death. Nicholas and the others fled with their lives. The execution was awful." He shuddered.

"Executions aren't unusual in Eastbourne. The murderers and rebels are put to death in the square. Why would Nicholas and the others run?"

"The Church is calling for blood. I can't do this anymore. It was one thing to be Master Wycliffe's assistant at Oxford, but this is getting out of hand." The man sounded hysterical.

"Repingdon!" Isaac had him by his shoulders. "You're not making sense. Why did the others run?"

He wouldn't meet Isaac's eye. "Peter was killed, right along with those criminals."

I bit my lip to keep from crying out.

"Are you certain?" Isaac asked.

"I was there." he promised. "It was a horrible sight."

Isaac's eyes narrowed. "Then why are you still here?"

Repingdon backed toward the door.

"Why haven't you run?"

"There wasn't time to run!" he cried. "I had to make a deal."

Isaac halted in his steps. "What did you do?" The double doors flew open, and guards poured in, surrounding him. Isaac fought and struggled, but it was no use. The satchel fell from his shoulder, but the guards didn't notice. They bound his wrists together and led him outside. The door shut behind them, and everything was still. Repingdon sat curled into a miserable ball on the floor. He stood up shaking and noticed the satchel on the floor.

Leave it. I thought. *You've done enough.*

He stared at it for a moment before picking it up and examining the contents. His gaze moved to the rusted crucifix at the front of the church. "I didn't have a choice!" he cried. With that, he stepped out the door and was gone.

—⚏—

I followed them at a distance. They entered the city and led Isaac to the center of town. I crept down an alleyway, listening.

"This is the man." said a deep, familiar voice.

"We found him in the abandoned chapel, Father Jacob."

"Was there any sign of her?" he asked in a mournful voice.

"I'm afraid not, Father."

He let out a grieved cry. "You wicked beast!"

I peered out of the alley to see him strike Isaac.

"What have you done to her?"

Isaac met his gaze. "Protected her from you."

A brief, victorious smile passed over the face of my uncle, then disappeared. "I don't know what you mean." He turned to the guards. "Take him to prison. He shall be questioned in the morning."

I sighed, relieved that they were not going to kill him, at least not yet.

Before the guards took him away, my uncle pulled one of

them aside and led him toward the alley. I backed farther into the darkness, praying that I wouldn't be seen.

"Please search the chapel again." he begged, pitifully. "If Colt's here, she's can't be far." His voice took on a pleading. "She's all the family that I have."

"Of course, Father."

It was a sickening performance, but the soldier believed it and headed down the street.

I took several steps backward, when my foot caught on something in the dark alley. My arms thrashed in every direction, looking for something to grip, but I went tumbling into a stack of crates

"Who's back there?" he called.

I could hear him groping his way down the dark alley. Pushing myself to my feet, I could hear him drawing closer. Hiding was over. It was time to run.

Chapter 14

"Elizabeth!" I heard my name echo off of the walls behind me. The alley opened up onto the streets, and I broke into a run. I glanced behind me, without slowing my pace, and saw my uncle emerge from the alley, his priestly robes shining in the sunset's light. I turned back just in time to notice a peddlers cart pushed just a bit too far into the street. I tried to swerve around it, but it was too late. I tripped trying to avoid it and hit the ground. I lay there, stunned for a moment. Turning, I saw my uncle at the end of the street. I jumped to my feet and bolted for the gates. Outside of Eastbourne, I realized I couldn't run much longer. Yet there was nowhere to hide. Out of the corner of my eye, I spied a path hardly worn and diving into thick woods. A memory whispered in a back corner of my mind. I knew where this path led. Running as hard as I could, I felt my feet surge forward and carry me the extra distance to my hiding place. When I reached it, I hit the doorstep and flew forward landing face down in the Old House of Curses.

I lay there gasping for breath. With the exhaustion came tears. I convulsed with sobs. I was alone. Truly, there was no one. Isaac, Peter, Alice, and my parents were all gone in different ways. When the sobbing had stopped, I remembered how thirsty I was. Sitting up, I saw that the sun had disappeared under the horizon, and I longed for someone, anyone to come and rescue me. As this thought came to mind a sound caught my attention. Rain. How often I had despised it, but now it was a welcome comfort. The sound was company to me. Pulling myself to my feet, I peered outside and in the mist, I beheld a man walking up the path. My breath caught in my throat and, backing deeper within the house, I hid myself behind a pile of blackened wreckage, not even daring to breathe.

Footsteps pounded on the floor, accompanied by heavy breathing. I tried to slow my thundering heart, and clenched my hands into fists to stop their shaking. The heavy breathing slowed to a regular pace, and no one called out. Perhaps, he had not seen me. I waited. Not a sound.

Scrape…

The noise made me jump. It was like two stones being struck together.

"*Filii solvet reddere enim Pater peccatum.*" My uncle's voice hissed from the front room.

I was trembling all over. He knew I was here. So, why didn't he just find me and have it over with?

The scraping sounded again, and I realized it was the familiar sound of my uncle starting a fire. Soon, I could see the light of it, dancing on the walls.

"Come out." he called. "No use in torturing yourself."

I didn't move.

"You're all alone out here, aren't you?"

Silence.

"It's such a shame when they all abandon you, isn't it?"

"What do you want from me?" I screamed, standing up from behind my barrier.

He smiled, his fat figure made massive as he sat in firelight. This had been his plan all along. He clicked his tongue. "Now, now, keep your temper."

"Why are you here?" I cried; my voice shrill.

"You can't figure that out for yourself?"

My lips trembled as I stepped toward him. "There is nothing left for you to take away. Why can't you just leave me alone?"

His eyes widened. "I told you that I would find you wherever you were. You did this to yourself."

"What?" I stared, disbelieving.

"I had nothing to do with your decision." He shrugged.

I glared at him accusingly. "Who told my parents I was dead?"

His gaze traveled slowly upward. "They wouldn't have left if they had known you were here."

"Who arrested Isaac Colt?"

"He was a man worthy of death."

"Who killed Peter Lockton?"

He laughed. "So you've heard the news. England is safer with such an evil gone from among us."

"How could you?" I had the sudden urge to strangle him.

He held up his hands in defense. "No, not me. It was by the king's decree. The king's soldiers carried out the act. Take it up with him, if you're so passionate."

My throat tightened. "Why do you seek to destroy me?"

His eyes returned to their saucer-like state. "Destroy you? Why, no, that's not how I remember it at all. In fact, I offered to help you when we met in Eastbourne, and you ran away."

"Because you wanted to kill me."

"No!" He stood to his feet. "It was because the guilty flee though no one pursues them."

It was my turn to stare, wide eyed. "Then, that is who I am to you. That is who I have always been. 'The guilty', 'The criminal', 'The wicked'. You must be thrilled to have finally caught me."

"You little fool! Do you think I've been ignorant of your plotting? Do you think I've not had my eye on you the whole time?"

"If you have always known, then why did you not arrest me?"

"What charge would I have to arrest you?"

I realized then that Master Repingdon had left out an extremely valuable piece of information. My uncle did not know that I was the writer.

"You see, Elizabeth, I have only tried to help you."

"You wish me to believe that?"

He looked to the right and then to the left as if searching for a crowd. "You have no one. Where will you run, if not to me?"

"There are others." I said lamely.

"And where are they? Colt, Lockton, they're not here. Even Alice Fitton, wherever she is, has abandoned you." His glee triumphed over me.

I stared at the ground, unable to answer.

He was watching me intently. "Then, you truly are all alone."

I nodded.

"Well then, I make you one last offer. I will pretend this nightmare never happened if you give it me."

"Give what to you?"

"The illegal translation, written by Isaac Colt."

"But you have it!" I cried.

He tilted his head, confused. "If I had it, why would I come to you looking for it?"

"But I saw it!" I protested. "I give you my word! It was in the bag."

"You word means nothing to me. You are the daughter of a cheat and a liar, cursed since the day you were born!" He was beginning to lose control. "You've been hiding out with thieves and criminals for weeks. Look at what they've done to you! You're poisoned by their heresy. It's a good thing that your parents think you dead. Imagine the shame they would feel at seeing you now!" He sent a furious look toward the fire. "Come tomorrow with the translation. I'm sure Isaac Colt will want to see you." He rose from his spot, stepped out the door, and fled into the storm.

—⁕—

I paced as the thunder roared outside. What was I to do? He was sure I had the translation. How was I to convince him otherwise? Something in me was burning. Why did he hate me so? What had I done? This wasn't just about the translation. He had hated me my whole life, but why?

Lighting flashed, and across the room I saw a face. "Who's there?" I called over the thunder, looking about me for something with which to arm myself. I was not alone, yet the other person neither called out nor made a sound. I stood perfectly still, listening. Who else would take refuge in the House of Curses? "Is someone there?" No answer. I reached for one of the boards and took a wary step forward. My own hands were shaking. Lighting split the sky again, illuminating the face. It was as frightened as my own. Only when it was dark again did I realize it *was* my own. My reflection had caught on a metal disk hanging on the wall. It was a mirror made of polished silver. I had heard of the rich owning such trinkets, but had never seen one for myself. I moved toward the darkened wall to be sure. When I reached it, the lighting flashed again. In one moment, I saw what I had been blind to for so long. Peter's eyes were staring back at me like translucent blue flames.

—⁓—

I stole toward the village near midnight, the moon lighting my path before me. Eastbourne was empty and silent as I darted along the streets toward the alleyway. It was a different place at night and much harder to navigate. The translation had to be somewhere.

I darted through the city gates when something drew my attention. The moonlight shone white in the little graveyard. I didn't want to go in. It was better if I didn't know. Yet, I pushed myself toward the iron fence, behind which, many tombstones were set in rows. One in particular gleamed in the moonlight. My breath came in shallow gasps as I knelt down, and reached between the iron bars until my fingers brushed the name and epitaph.

Margaret Lockton
Died 1367
Maledictus

My lips trembled. Chills tiptoed up my scalp the same way they had when I had seen my reflection. *1367...* Fifteen years ago. The year I was born.

Margaret. That was the name the mad woman in the street had screamed at me. I didn't want to believe it. It couldn't be true. Yet, here it was. Margaret was my mother. At the unspoken truth, my eyes filled with tears. Yet, it was Peter's name that I heard myself sobbing. Burying my face in my hands, I could only think of question after question. Who was she? How had they died? I remembered Peter talking of his father only once. My hands flew to the gold chain at my neck. Peter's father, my father, had created this. Is that why Peter had given it to me? Had it been meant for me? No answers. The moonlight was silent. I gently pressed the chilled golden leaf to my face, when a hand rested on my shoulder.

I pulled back, screaming, and twisted around, only to have the hand seal my mouth shut. My back was pressed against the iron fence.

"Quiet." the dark figure, commanded in a hoarse whisper.

Without pulling his hand away from my mouth he reached up and removed his hood. His blue eyes shone in the silver light, like living ice. Peter slowly withdrew his hand from my mouth.

I stumbled forward, and he caught me by the shoulders. "I don't understand." I gasped breathlessly.

He grinned. "You called."

"But what are you doing here?"

The light faded from his face. "Do you want to know the truth?"

I shook my head in an emphatic *No*, then looked up at him. "Yes."

"I'm Chancley's spy."

Ripping away from him, I nearly lost my balance, but he caught my hand.

I stopped my struggling, and stared at him, my eyes narrowed.

"Please don't think me a traitor. I had to follow his every whim or he might have hurt you."

"So, you're partners now?" I shot back. "I'm sure he tells you all of his brilliant plans for me."

Pain scarred his features. "Your uncle knows how to exact the perfect torture. I was given no choice." His jaw tightened. "He promised me that if I were ever to speak or reveal myself to you, a soldier would be standing near and would kill you before your next breath."

"Then, what are you doing here?"

"Tonight my guards prefer the tavern to a cold, empty street."

"Chancley seems to have all of the soldiers under his thumb." I muttered.

"Yes." Peter agreed. "And they are deadly shots. I still tried to get to you."

I remembered the figure who had saved from Alice Fitton's crumbling home. "You pulled me from the fire."

He nodded.

My lips began to tremble. "I thought you were dead."

"I know. So does everyone else. Chancley found an innocent man who bore my resemblance and executed him in the square, calling him by my name. The crowd didn't know the difference. I would have gladly taken his place."

"Why did he do that? He has you prisoner. If he wanted to make a public example of you, he could have."

"He was waiting."

"Waiting for what?"

"Waiting for you. He doesn't want just me, he wants us both; a matched set."

"Why?"

"Because he believes we're a curse on his existence, and that the curse will end when we do."

"If someone should see us—"

"I know." he sighed. "But I had to speak with you. Chancley may spare you if you can give him the translation."

"I don't have it!"

"Shh!" He held a finger to his lips.

"Phillip Repingdon, the one who betrayed us, took it."

Peter's face went pale. "He's gone. Chancley sent him to London, to recant."

"Recant?"

"Repent of his heresy. It's likely that he took the translation with him to burn it and show his sincerity."

"Then it's gone." Tears filled my eyes. "It might have been easier to bear what's coming if I knew it was safe."

"You've changed." He studied me.

"Yes, I have."

His eyes shone. "Tell me someday."

"I promise. I hope you have enough time to hear it all the way through."

"Elizabeth." he whispered. "If nothing else, we have eternity." He turned and donned the hood once again. "I need to go."

"Peter." I called.

He stopped and looked back at me.

"Why did you come looking for me?"

A smile lit his face, and kneeling down, he pointed at the gravestone. "Because I made a promise to my Mother that I would take care of her baby."

He stood to his feet, and we looked at one another. I stepped forward and threw my arms around him with tears streaming down my cheeks. He held me as I cried. "I'm so afraid." I gasped between sobs.

"I know." He choked back tears. "So am I."

I stepped back, and he leaned down. "Take courage and be strong. Do not be afraid of them, and do not be discouraged for the Lord thy God is with you wherever you go."

The words filled my soul. "That's beautiful."

"Our father translated it from a Hebrew manuscript. He quoted it often. He lived and died by it. That's why Chancley believed he was a curse."

"There is so much I want to know about them."

He glanced from side to side. "Follow me."

He led me down a side street until we reached a shack by the water. The walls had rotted away. He led me into the building where the heavy dust we had disturbed caused us both to erupt in spasms of coughing. "What is this place?" I asked when my coughing had subsided.

He turned to me and grinned. "Our father's workshop."

In the middle of the room was a melting pot, and at the desk there were rusted tools, and all sorts of rocks.

"He was a goldsmith. He and Isaac used to work here."

"Isaac?"

"Isaac was apprenticed to him."

I looked up at him. "Thank you for bringing me here."

"After they were killed, no one came here. No one tore it down. Chancley, who was the priest here, forced them to keep it up as a reminder of the family who was destroyed in their sin."

My gaze was travelling along the walls, when I noticed something at Peter's feet that did not belong. My heart leapt and I was about to tell Peter, when the words came to me, "*Take courage, and be strong...*" In that moment, I made my decision. "Peter!" I gasped. "We need to leave."

He stared at me. "Why?"

"Because," I searched for an answer. "Because it's nearly dawn. Chancley will be looking for you."

He hung his head. "You're right."

We stole up the street in the darkness, and at the gates we stopped.

"Promise me that you'll tell me about them."

"Someday." He cleared his throat.

I leaned closer, with urgency. "Someday soon."

He embraced me, and when we pulled back, tears shone in his eyes. He grasped my fingers once more and disappeared down the road.

"Thank you for finding me." I whispered as he turned into the shadows.

—⚬—

I knelt in the little workshop, listening to the sound of the waves. I clasped my hands together and looked through the crumbling ceiling at the stars. "I am not brave." I whispered. "But

I will obey You." I remembered a line from the prayer I had heard the translators pray. "And, Lord, give us, Thy poor sheep, patience and strength to suffer for Thy law. I ask this now, for more need was there never." Strength tamed my pounding heart. "In the Name of Jesus, Amen." The words washed over me like music.

Chapter 15

The morning light burned through the pale mist. I took one step, then another toward the Old House of Curses. When I reached the base of the hill I saw My uncle already at the top, and had the urge to turn back. Suddenly, I remembered the next verse of my mother's lullaby. The words gave me the strength to move. I stepped forward with my shoulders back, my face into the rain-streaked wind, and began to sing.

"And when you are afraid, my darling, when you are afraid
If worry claims you for her own if darkness shrieks your name
Take courage then, my dearest love, for though you cannot see
Our God is watching over you, He'll bring you back to me"

I reached the top of the hill to see him glaring at me, and for the slightest of moments, I saw terror in his eyes before he recovered himself. "You have not run." he said, surprised.

"And I shall not."

"You do not have the translation." The words slipped between gritted teeth.

"I told you that yesterday, and you did not believe me."

He raised his eyebrows. "Well then," He turned to look behind him.

Two guards emerged from the house with their faces hidden under helmets. Between them, they led a man bound at the wrists. He lifted his head and winced when he saw me. This man was not the same Isaac Colt that I had seen the day before. He was defeated and cowed by these men, his face beaten and bruised. They led him behind Chancley, to the other side of me. They halted him, and kicked him to his knees, enjoying themselves.

"Master Colt." Chancley delivered a sweeping bow. His eyes were thin slits of triumph. "Now, one of you knows where the manuscripts are." The priest paced in front of us. "I have given you both equal chances to repent. Neither of you will."

Isaac glanced at me out of the corner of his eye and stared back at the ground.

"Master Colt, where are the forbidden manuscripts?"

"If I had them, do you think we'd be here?" he muttered. A guard kicked his side, and he crouched low to the ground.

"Elizabeth." Chancley turned to me. "Where is the translation?"

My throat tightened. "I told you everything I knew yesterday."

"I thought as much. Let us begin."

He nodded to the soldiers, and one of them laid hold of me, dragging me toward the house. Screaming, I fought and struggled to no avail. The soldiers bound my hands behind a pillar of the Old House of Curses.

"Set it ablaze." the cleric rumbled.

"Let her go!" Isaac pleaded. "She doesn't know anything."

Chancley laughed. "Oh, I know that. You see, it's not her I'm tormenting."

Isaac's eyes caught mine for one painful second. "I'll tell you anything you want to know."

"Good man." Chancley held up a hand, and the guards advanced no farther. "Now then, where are the manuscripts?"

Isaac bit his lip. "I don't know."

"I am beginning to lose my patience!" The priest lunged forward and struck Isaac, who lost his balance and fell to the ground.

I helplessly watched as they beat their defenseless victim. My throat burned as I struggled not to lose resolve. It was then that I remembered. I knew something that Chancley did not.

"Nevertheless, He is my shield, my strength and my salvation!" I cried; my voice hoarse.

Chancley stopped, and turned to look at me

"And I shall be moved no more."

"What nonsense is this?" he asked breathlessly.

"I have it, Chancley. I have the manuscript."

"What?" He stood and stalked over to me. "How can that be?"

I stared at him, his face inches away from mine. "I remember everything I write."

"You?" he laughed.

I interrupted his cackling. "What makes you think that Master Colt wrote the translation? Look at him!"

The guards pulled Isaac back up to his knees. His eyes were wide with fear.

"Have you seen his hands? The man can't write his own name!"

"Elizabeth!" Isaac shouted. "What are you doing?"

I watched Father Jacob. His face writhed and twisted with indecision, then set in a grim line. "Let her be burned." His voice trembled with rage.

"Chancley!" Isaac cried. "She's lying. I'm the writer! Take your wrath out on me."

The soldiers did not move at the priest's command but wavered.

"I said I want her dead!" he screamed.

The guards jumped to work at tightening the ropes on my hands.

"Wait." Chancley called when they had finished. "Not just her. Burn the whole house. Burn all that remains. Let her die a death befitting her."

"You would murder a child?" Isaac asked, incredulous.

"This 'Child' would not live if it were not for me! Her life is mine to give and take!"

"Every life is God's!"

The cleric said nothing in reply but walked toward me. In his hand was the flint. He struck a spark to his right. The dry wood caught, instantly, and the flames began to claw their way up the walls. He struck to the left, and it did the same. One of the soldiers helped him by lighting fires throughout the house. The other guarded Isaac, who now struggled viciously in his chains. "You can't do this!" he yelled.

"Isaac." I blinked back tears as he looked up. "It's alright."

He fought all the harder.

Jacob Chancley stepped over the threshold into the burning room. The air began to choke me with the stench of smoke. "Any last words, Miss Lockton?" he asked.

I met his gaze. "I am not who you say I am."

"After all I have done for you." he sighed. "I pulled you from the flames!" he hissed. "And I gave you a home with my barren sister and her husband! I thought as long as you were innocent, you could be free of your family's curse, but when your brother died at your hands, I knew better. Does the house look familiar, Elizabeth? Look around! This is what I saved you from, and you have come crawling back to die." He turned around and headed toward the door.

"The truth is worth dying for." I cried.

His head turned slightly. "And what truth is that? That you're a dishonorable wretch with parents who were struck down for their wickedness?"

"No. That God didn't hate me. You did. He didn't try to hurt me at every turn. You did." My voice rose. "And God didn't kill my parents!" My eyes widened with the realization. "You did."

"I was only a tool."

"In whose hands?"

"That question," he laughed. "Will die with you." He neared the door, only as a pile of burning debris crashed down in front of it, blocking his way. He spun to glare at me as if I had willed it to happen. He scoured the wall, and the room for another way out, but there was none, except a hole, not nearly large enough for him. He sank to his knees in defeat.

"Who burned this house?" I yelled over the roaring blaze around us. "Who burned Isaac Colt's home, or Alice Fitton's?"

"Silence!" he shouted, standing to his feet. I could see the fear on his face. He was terrified.

I closed my eyes. "Take courage and be strong."

He stepped toward me. "I will take this no longer!" Kicking my feet out from under me, he reached for a thick shard of glass at his feet, and raised it high. As I watched him, a realization struck me and I looked him in the eye. "Kill me, but know this; I am not afraid to die." I twisted toward the wall and kicked it in. Sparks flew around me, and I closed my eyes as the rubble fell. In that moment, death was no longer a dark chasm. It was a door, a door to the light, and the fresh air, where all of my fears would be gone, and all of my questions answered. I waited for the searing pain but felt nothing. I opened my eyes to see the wall, just above me, balanced against the column I was bound to. All around me, the ground was ablaze, and out from under the rubble lay the still hand of the priest.

"Elizabeth!" Isaac called through the opening.

"Yes!" I coughed.

"I'm going to get you out!"

"Hurry!" I could feel the consciousness fading from me.

"I'll kick in the front wall." he shouted.

"No! You can't! The ceiling is going to crumble. It won't take that." I glanced up to see the flames, starting to descend the pillar to which I was bound, and I formed a plan. I stretched forward, pulling myself as far from the pillar as possible, and pressed my hands into fists. I screamed, feeling the fire engulf my hands. The ropes disintegrated and snapped. Stumbling toward the opening, I realized that I would barely fit through it. I was nearly to the hole, when someone cried out. I stopped just short of the doorway. It was coming from another room in the house.

"Elizabeth!" Isaac called from outside. "What are you doing?"

I held hand up to silence him. The shouting started again and faded away. "Do you hear that?"

"Get out of there!" he cried, gripping my hand.

"No, Isaac!" I fought him.

"You're not thinking clearly!" He pulled harder, but I wrenched backward.

"Isaac, don't you understand? He's in here, somewhere."

"What are you talking about?"

"Isaac, he wants the 'Matched Set'." Reaching for the gold chain at my neck, I pulled with all my strength until it broke free, and threw it out the opening. "The goldsmith's shop. That's where you'll find the translation." With that, I turned and ran into the blaze.

I flew through the room, hardly able to see.

Peter's words rang in my head.

I ducked down a hallway, and as I did, the ceiling behind me gave way. I was just seconds ahead of the collapse.

He doesn't want just me. He's waiting...

I turned into a room and knelt to the ground, where the smoke was not so thick.

Waiting for the Matched Set. Chancley had been after two prizes in this.

I saw a limp body bound and gagged.

"Peter!" I shrieked over the roar and crackle of the fire.

He didn't move.

I tore at the rope but could not loosen it. I pulled with all my might, unable to put conscious thought into my movements any longer. I searched the room and saw all of the smoke flowing to one place; a shattered window. Dragging his body toward the window, I hesitated only a moment. Then by some unknown Strength, I lifted him and shoved him through the window. With one last look about, I pushed myself up on the window sill. The remaining glass cut into my hands. I saw the bleeding but felt nothing. Shadows crept into my line of vision. The corners became blurry and blotted. I felt myself falling, saw the flames above me, and gave in to the darkness.

Chapter 16

And when we meet again, my darling, when we meet again
Although it be on distant shores though life has met its end
No sweeter joy shall find my heart, no day will greater be
I'll thank the God, Who found us both,
Who brought you back to me

———

Back, forth. The motion made me want to vomit. Back, forth. I opened my eyes to a darkened room. Looking down, I saw that my hands were bound in bandages. Back and forth. I leaned over the bed to heave, but nothing happened. I rolled back over, and every part of my body complained. My stomach was empty.

A door opened, and Isaac Colt stood in the doorway. "Do you remember me?" he teased.

I opened my mouth to speak, and the dry aching of my throat prevented it. So, I just smiled.

He came closer, holding a cup of water to my lips. The iciness trickled down my throat, and I found my scratchy voice. "I feel awful."

"I know." He nodded. "But you've had one of the best physicians I have ever met."

"You?" I asked.

He laughed. "No. Do you think I would have gotten either of you out of there in one piece?"

I shook my head, when I remembered. "Where's Peter?"

"In far better shape than you." A voice boomed from the doorway.

I turned to see John Atlee step into the room. Yet, to me, he was known by only one name. "Father!"

He came to my side, and checked the cuts and burns on my hands while Isaac went to sit with Peter. "How do you feel?" my father asked.

I only looked at him, knowing my face answered the question.

He laughed. "As I expected."

"How did you find me?" I wondered.

He set himself back in a chair. "That is far too long a story for so tired a someone."

"Where are we?"

"Shh," he quieted. "No more questions. You need to sleep."

I nodded, but was unable to coax myself into doing so. My eyes were wide open, and my mind was alive with questions. "I can't."

He scooted the chair closer. "Then close your eyes, and listen."

I eyed him suspiciously, then obeyed.

"Several years ago, there was a young married couple." His voice was quiet and soothing. "They loved one another, and prayed desperately that the Lord above would grant them children. They prayed until it became apparent that they would never receive such a blessing."

I began to drift away, yet the story did not grow more distant, but instead it played in my head like actors on a stage.

"Then one day, as they prayed there was a knock at the door. They opened it to find a priest on the doorstep, holding a newborn girl."

He paused looking to see if I had drifted off to sleep. I did not pretend otherwise.

Then he whispered, quite close to me. "So you see, my Bethy, you are no one's curse. You are my answered prayer."

—⁂—

When I awoke again, I was alone in the same dark room. There was no one to talk to, so instead, I thought. Events, faces, and truths rolled in my mind. One shouted above all the others. *Peter is my brother.* I laughed at how long it had taken me to discover. Dear Peter. He had not given up on me. A thought struck me with such force that it was several moments before I remembered to breathe. Alice. She was my grandmother as well as Peter's. She had known of course. I wanted my heart to split in two, so great was the war of feeling. Such a fear overcame me at the thought of not seeing her again. What if she did not recover? The grief struck me with surprising force. Yet oh, how much more I loved her. I wanted to clasp her hands and cry on her shoulder.

"It's time to leave." My father shut the door behind him.

"So soon?"

He laughed. "We've been on this ship all day, and for most of the night."

I sat up a bit. "Ship?"

"Yes, to Dieppe. The ship has just docked, and unless you wish to go back to Eastbourne, we should get off."

"Of course." I moved to get up.

He stopped me. "Slowly."

When I sat up, searing pain shot through my back. I stepped one foot out of bed without any ill side effects. The other followed. Then Father gave me his hands and counted to three. I set my teeth and stood. I was not much better than a cripple. Everything hurt for one reason or another, and the feeling haunted me that I might be like this forever.

I stepped off of the ship leaning most of my weight on my father. As we descended, I saw Peter waiting for us. I had the urge to run down the plank to greet him but thought better of it. The moment my feet touched solid ground Peter threw his arms about my shoulders. I laughed, but he didn't laugh back. His grip was tight, and out of the corner of my eye I saw his jaw tremble. He stepped back, tears slipping down his cheeks.

I touched his hand. "I'm alright." I promised.

He nodded. "You should have listened to Isaac, and not put yourself in danger for me."

I smiled up at him. "I could give you the same lecture." I looked about. "Where is Isaac?"

My father looked sober. "He didn't come."

"But I saw him." I insisted.

"He helped me to find a ship and boarded it with us, but he said that he had business to take care of."

My stomach tightened a bit. Couldn't all of it stop for just a moment or two?

"How is Mother?" I was afraid to ask.

A tired look came to his face, and my heart stopped. "She is weak."

I sighed with relief.

He nodded. "She has been a different person since learning of your death. She begged me not to leave her, but I could not explain why I had to go just in case it was all a trick."

"How did you know to come?" I asked.

"Isaac Colt sent word to me." As he said this, the three of us turned the corner onto a tight, cobbled street. There in the second story window, I caught a glimpse of my mother. Her face drained of color at seeing me. I smiled at her, and she fled from the window. The door on the street opened, and she enveloped me with tears flowing. She sobbed my name over and over again holding me tighter with every moment.

"Oh, Dear Lord, is this a dream like all the others?" she cried.

"I promised you wouldn't lose me." I sobbed, my voice muffled in her shoulder.

—⊠—

The house was small but lovely, nestled in a corner of the French countryside.

"We purchased it the day before I got word." My father smiled proudly on it.

Without much assistance, I was able to limp across the field to where it sat. We had spent a fortnight in town with an acquaintance of my parents, but the city was a harsh, loud, unnatural thing to all of us. Now, we were away from the noise and in the quiet of the country.

My father's study was only a tiny room with nothing but a mortar and pestle in one corner. "Quite a laboratory." I observed, stepping in.

"It's not much, but we'll build onto it." He stretched, looking around the room.

I smiled, but it faded quicker than I had intended.

"Perhaps we ought to talk." he suggested. "Your friend Isaac told me very little of your time as a translator."

We stepped into the warm July afternoon and strolled

through the surrounding woods. Over the next hour, I unburdened myself. He listened, saying nothing at all.

"What did I do to cause all of this?" I asked, finally.

He gently began to guide our steps back toward the house. "Nothing. You were born into it."

"Because of who my parents were?"

"That's not what I said. You were born with a purpose, far beyond anything we can know. Trouble will follow you. It always follows those who take a stand for what is right, but you will bear it."

We stayed silent for several moments, stepping inside and returning to his study.

He eyed me. "Something still troubles you."

"No." I shook my head, twisting a lock of hair around my index finger.

He didn't speak, and didn't force me to. Yet, I could feel him waiting for my answer.

My eyes shot upward and met his. "What am I supposed to do now?"

He looked at me, steadily. "Live today. Then, live tomorrow. Then, live the next day, and if God wants you to do more than that, He'll show you."

—m—

The days flew by like the fluttering pages of a book left in the breeze. Peter again, became my father's apprentice, and a permanent part of our family. After all that had happened, some might have found this life boring, but we welcomed it. My father took me on his rounds, and I discovered that I was not any good with the sick. Though I lacked the qualities of a physician, I soon found that there was another gift which I possessed. I could play with children. There were so many in the filthy crowded streets. When adults were ill, my job became holding infants, singing lullabies, or telling stories to their children. It was an occupation which I excelled in, and it gave me such satisfaction.

To my delight, I soon found out that Sybil Garret was living with her Aunt in a town not far from ours. We saw each other often, and though much in each of us had changed, our closeness with one another had not. Perhaps that is the way of friendships which start in a graveyard.

It seemed that this was my life now. No more translating, and no more being hunted down. This didn't upset me. I was content to live life and enjoy every moment. What worried me, was that as the weeks passed, there was no word from England and no sign of Isaac Colt or Alice Fitton. Often, someone would pass me in the street and my heart would quicken, only to find that I had been mistaken. Every time I saw someone suffering in pain, or in a fever I would think of Alice, and wondered if she had ever recovered. I knew it bothered Peter as well, though he never said so.

I longed to ask Peter more about the mother and father I knew so little about. Yet, I was frightened at the thought. So often, I had wanted answers, and now that they were right in front of me, I was terrified to reach out and touch them.

One morning I woke long before dawn and stepped outside into the dewy morning. I watched the horizon unsure of when the sun would rise, when I heard the front door shut gingerly. Peter stepped out of the house.

"Did I wake you?" I whispered.

"No, I couldn't sleep."

We both watched the eastern sky for some time until he turned to me, cheeks red from the cold. "Are you ready to know?"

I watched the clouds on the horizon, studying them. "Yes."

He placed a hand on my shoulder. "I loved our parents very much. They taught me to read and write and pray. And I prayed for only one thing."

"What?"

"What else would a seven year old pray for?" He grinned. "A playmate. I must have been the only child in the village without a brother or sister. Mother told me that she had prayed for the same thing. So, I prayed every night. Soon, my parents told me my prayer was to be answered. I still prayed, but now it was for someone specific."

I smiled to myself.

"One night, I woke to horrid sounds from down the hall. I asked my father what was wrong, and he replied that nothing was amiss and that I ought to go outside. It was summer, so it was warm and dry outside. I remember falling asleep while staring up at the stars. I woke several hours later to smoke and flames. I was too frightened to attempt running into the house. So, I stood watching as my home burned to the ground. A window shattered.

My mother, pulled herself out of that window with one arm, clutching a bundle in her arms. I ran to her, but there was nothing I could do. She held out a screaming baby and placed her in my hands. Then, she looked me in the eye and said, 'Promise me that you'll look after her.'" Peter stopped.

I didn't know what to say. My eyes misted as I stared at the eastern mountains. "Then, you kept your promise."

He nodded. "Those were her last words. There is nothing worse a child could go through than to watch a parent suffer like that. I sat there, staring at the baby, wondering what to do, and then from the shadows, stepped a man, whom I knew to be the village priest. I begged him not to take the baby. I struggled and fought against him."

"What did he do?"

"He didn't do anything. I was seven, and a scrawny seven, at that. He knew I would follow him as long as he had you, and I suppose I did."

"You suppose?"

Peter nodded. "Looking over my shoulder to see my mother was the last thing I remember."

"What happened?" I ventured.

"I don't know. The memories just aren't there. I remember thinking about the promise I had made, and how I had failed. My grandmother told me that there had been no baby when the priest had arrived with me. I had to assume that you had died, but I knew I would be restless until I found the priest and asked him."

"Then, Alice raised you?" The name brought a smile to my face.

"Yes, our mother was her daughter."

The sun reached up over the horizon, and caressed the landscape with warmth as we headed for the house.

"When did you come looking for me?" I asked.

"When I left Oxford, I had hoped to continue helping Master Wycliffe with his work in Lutterworth, but he said no. He knew my heart was somewhere else. So he told me to go take care of whatever unfinished business was holding me back. The only place I knew to go was Eastbourne. I found the remains of my old home. I was amazed that it had not been torn down after all this time. The townspeople thought it to be cursed. I went there anyway."

"Is that where you met Isaac?"

"Yes. I remember him telling me that he had to stay in the House of Curses so that God could strike him down. So, I got to know him, and showed him a little bit of what I knew about God."

"From what he said, it was more than a little to him. You saved his life."

"Well, he's done the same for me, several times over."

We were quiet for several moments.

"Do you think Isaac and Alice are alright?" I asked.

"They're in God's hands." he replied.

"So, how did you find Tonbridge?"

"After knowing Isaac for some time, and remembering him as

my father's apprentice, I told him why I had come to Eastbourne. He told me that the priest I was searching for had recently taken a parish in Tonbridge, and advised me not to search for him."

"And you didn't listen." I couldn't hold back the smile. "What was he to do with us?"

Peter laughed. "He tried to warn me, but I wouldn't listen. I found out all that I could about the small community, and left on foot to find Chancley. I met Lord Garret, who I knew to be a friend of Wycliffe. He told me that the priest had gone to Eastbourne just days before, and I might have even passed him on the way. The weather was too unpredictable for me to try and go back the way I had come, but he also told me that the priest had a sister outside the village, who might let me board with her family through the winter storms. He told me quite a bit about them, and where I could find their home. So, I started out the next morning, and was caught in a very unforgiving storm."

"You didn't know I was Chancley's niece."

He shook his head. "Not until I woke up to find my own eyes staring back at me."

"Did Isaac come with you?"

"No, he had gone to Oxford earlier that winter because I had written Master Wycliffe on his behalf. Alice was there, and when they went nearly all winter without hearing from me, they came looking for me. They arrived in Tonbridge, just before I had to leave."

I stared upward, amazed at his story.

"Nothing broke my heart more than not telling you. I wanted to so much, but Chancley had threatened your parents, saying that if you knew, it would curse you."

"I wasn't ready to know."

"So many times, I regretted coming in the first place."

"No." I set my hand on his. "It was supposed to happen just as it did. Everything had a reason. If you hadn't come I would never have known. If you hadn't left, I would never have had the chance to write." I smiled. "You should have seen Isaac's face when he got your message."

"What message?"

"The one that you sent in your letter. The one about me writing for them."

"I never said that."

"You did." I insisted, standing up. "Stay there." I went into the house, came back a few moments later holding the pages that had lasted with me for so long. I flipped to the last page. "Tell Colt you have what he needs." I quoted.

Peter shook his head. "And Isaac thought that meant I wanted you write for them?"

I nodded, searching his face. "Isn't that what it meant?"

Peter looked at me, trying not to laugh. "Elizabeth, Isaac needed the Latin for the last ten Psalms." He turned the letter over, and I saw the Latin manuscript. It had been with me all along.

—⁓—

I sat down across from my mother as she sorted plants on the table. She had been picking herbs and flowers from the valley that evening. She smiled as I sat down and fingered through the plants, knowing specifically the purpose for each one. The mint, the lavender, and the chamomile, all had many purposes. Her favorite, however, was to make a simple tea. I found one bloom which I could not name.

"What is this?" I asked while sniffing the delicate white blossom.

"White Campion." she answered.

"What is it for?"

"Well, I don't know of any medicinal value, but it was so lovely I had to pick it."

I smiled at this sudden break away from my mother's practical nature. "It's beautiful."

She set her calloused hand on mine. "You're changed." she murmured, almost to herself.

"I am." I nodded. "But I love you no less."

She smiled, but it faded. "I must know, Bethy. Are you angry?"

I weighed my answer, as carefully as any merchant weighs his cost. "Not at you."

"I understand."

"I don't wish to be angry, but how long will it take to forgive?"

"A lifetime, Dear." She smiled sadly. "I'm so sorry we kept this from you. God forgive me if I erred."

I shook my head and stared upward, trying to fight tears. "No." I bit my lip, wondering if I should ask the question that pounded in my mind. "Did you know her?"

"Only a little, before she met Richard Lockton. Jacob was in love with her, but when she married Richard he would have nothing to do with either of them. He told me never to speak with them. He accused them of heresy, among other things. John Atlee and Richard were close friends, but my brother made it quite clear that if John wanted anything to do with me, he would have to cut all connection with the Locktons. So, he did, and they were forgotten."

I let out a shaky breath, and looked up to see my mother's eyes sparkling with tears. I gave her hand a squeeze. "You know you will always be my mother." I whispered.

Her smile shone, as she wiped a tear from the corner of her eye.

"I am still so confused though. Does this mean another year of wearing black, mourning people I never knew?"

"A part of you will always grieve for them. But, as far as mourning is concerned," She set her hand on the dark sleeve of my dress. "Black is such a gloomy color." She reached again for the Campion blossom, and offered it to me. "You know the truth. Be free from sorrow."

After Mother had gathered up the plants, I stepped outside into the beautiful valley. The sky was a glorious array of gold and scarlet. Something came over me, and I wanted to run, and dance, and sing, and tell the world that God was good. I settled myself into the tall grass and gazed at the heavens. As I watched the first few stars come out, I closed my eyes and whispered. "Thank You, for finding me."

As I sat there searching the earthly sky for Heavenly answers I felt the assurance that one day I would see them again, but until then, there were many adventures to be had down here. The song rose in my heart and drifted over the meadow.

And when we meet again, my darling, when we meet again
Although it be on distant shores though life has met its end
No sweeter joy shall find my heart, no day will greater be
I'll thank the God, Who found us both,
Who brought you back to me

Epilogue

Winter set in that year bringing icy tidings. Peter surmised that if we were going to hear from Isaac, it wouldn't be until spring. So, I began to prepare myself for several more months of waiting and wondering.

My family found ways to bring relief to the poorer people in the town, many of whom my father had met on his rounds. We delivered food, quilts, and anything else that was needed to help see them through the winter. On one such day, I had set out by myself to take food to a family we knew. For me, nothing I did could replace writing, but feeding the hungry, or giving a blanket to someone's child held a similar satisfaction. It was the feeling I had wanted for so long. I had a purpose. I had been afraid that because of the burns on my hands, I would lose feeling in them as Isaac had. Sections had certainly been damaged, and scars were beginning to form, but the palms on my hands were nearly unaffected, since the fire had scorched my fists. I had been content here for some time, but something in me was still burning to be a part of the translation work. I had realized that when my hands had healed, but here, so far away from Master Wycliffe or any of the other translators, it seemed impossible.

As these thoughts were spinning through my head, I noticed something glinting on the frozen path in front of me. Setting my basket down, I knelt, and brushed away the flakes of snow to see a pendant, a golden leaf. My fingers trembled. I knew it all too well. Without taking my eyes from the pendant, I knew someone was standing in the alley, just to my left. "I hope you realize how late you are." I said.

He stepped out of the alley. "Perhaps by a few weeks."

"Months." I corrected.

"I'm sorry." He said, in a tone which was anything but sorry. "Is that all you have to say?"

I continued walking, trying to hide my smile. "No."

He caught up with me and kept in stride.

"You lied to me." I said without facing him.

He stopped, then tried to catch up with me. "Did I?"

I nodded. "You told me that you had made a promise to my father. Well, I talked to my father, and he said that until I disappeared, he'd never heard of you."

"He's speaks the truth, but then, so did I."

I stopped and stared up at him.

"I said I spoke to your father. I don't remember ever mentioning John Atlee's name."

I was speechless. So, Isaac had made a promise to Richard Lockton before I was even born. I looked at him, not sure what to say. A grin spread over my face. "You're still late." I continued down the street.

"Perhaps you'll forgive me." he called.

"What makes you think so?" I looked over my shoulder and saw Alice Fitton, standing next to him. The basket in my hand dropped. I ran toward her, and threw my arms around her. We cried, and hugged, and cried again. "We were so worried." I gasped. "Wait until Peter sees you."

"Child." She looked up at me, quite solemnly. "We've come to ask a favor."

I looked from one to the other.

"Most of Wycliffe's translators recanted in the fall, and we have a book that needs finishing. Master Wycliffe asked for both of you, specifically." Isaac grinned.

My heart thrilled. *Both of us.*

It had to be written. They had to know the truth. Someone had to set them free.

Afterword

I have heard people say that Historical Fiction, as a genre, is an oxymoron. How can one combine History as fact, and Fiction as make believe into one novel? In my opinion, there is no better way to study history, but in every Historical Fiction novel I have ever come across, the reader is left wondering how much of the story was real, and how much was a product of the author's imagination.

All of the main characters in this story were fictitious, many of them representing a certain class or people group. The Atlee family was an example of the rising middle class, not quite peasants, but nowhere near nobility. The Garret family represented the nobles, which normally would never have mingled with the lower classes. Jacob Chancley was a representation of the anger and unrest many felt about the Lollards and heretics of any kind. He is certainly not a blanket statement about the clergy of the day, but most bishops and priests who had any kind of influence were avid about the extinction of the Lollards. Peter Lockton, Isaac

Colt, and Alice Fitton portray those who followed the teaching and doctrines of John Wycliffe. Though they may have seemed few and far between, there were places in the country where, as one Lord said, "Every other man you meet in the street is a Lollard." The only real characters in this novel are Wycliffe and his companions. Nicholas of Hereford, Phillip Repingdon, John Aston, and Lawrence Bedeman were all real men, all of whom eventually recanted their beliefs. Most of them made peace with the church in the fall of 1382 when this story takes place, but in order to show them in a correct light, we need to understand the kind of persecution they underwent.

In 1381, a revolt broke out known as the Peasants' Revolt. It was rumored that Wycliffe started the uprising. This, however, makes very little historical sense since one of Wycliffe's biggest supporters, John of Gaunt, lost nearly everything as a direct result of the uprising, and also because Wycliffe is known to have publicly disapproved of the revolt. All the same, the authorities needed someone to blame. In 1382, they began the persecution of the Lollards. Though never hurting Wycliffe directly, they pressured Oxford University to relieve him of his position, but the University did not. The church then began to persecute those closest to Wycliffe. In the summer of 1382, Nicholas of Hereford, Phillip Repingdon, John Aston, and Lawrence Bedeman were excommunicated from the church. This revoked their privileges at Oxford. It is likely that they were also cut off from society, being considered heretics. Though not practiced by the Catholic Church today, being excommunicated once included a practice known as the Civilia Jura (Civil Laws). Conversation, communication through letters, corporate prayer, and relationships of any nature were forbidden between the heretics and "the faithful". They were not even allowed to share a meal together. These men would have lost all contact with friends and family. Also, many of them faced imprisonment, which would have been a fate worse than death in the Middle Ages.

Repingdon, Aston, and Bedeman recanted in the fall of 1382. Nicholas, after pleading with the pope, enduring prison, harsh treatment, and watching his writings burned, recanted in 1391. We cannot say what these men were promised if they recanted, but each one was given at least a small rector's living. Nicholas eventually became the Chancellor of Hereford Cathedral in 1391. Repingdon was the Bishop of Lincoln by 1404.

Wycliffe himself lived to be about sixty-four, and died in 1384 of natural causes while pastoring a church in Lutterworth, Leicestershire, where he had retired from Oxford. It is not known just how much of the translation of the Scriptures he did himself, as much of the Old Testament was written by Nicholas of Hereford. John Purvey, a close friend of Wycliffe finished the translation after his death, and made revisions to the work, so that it would be more understandable. Wycliffe was not officially declared a heretic until 31 years after his death in the year 1415 by the Council of Constance. His bones were then exhumed, burned, and their ashes scattered on the River Swift as a warning to other Lollards.

None of the comments from these people in the story were

actual quotes except for the sections taken from the Lollard's prayer, when Wycliffe prays over the assembly of translators. I found this prayer by accident and fell in love with the simplicity of its request. However, due its length and complicated English I used only sections.

In my story, research was a difficult thing because so little is known about the common people of Fourteenth Century England. They worked to survive, and therefore, have little written history. The scholars and nobles that *did* record their own lives on paper obviously thought they had better things to do than write a biography on the lower classes. What we *do* know, however, is that the farmers and "serfs" of this age lived a literally third-world existence making their living conditions little better than that of slaves. Most of the common people were born on a plot of land, and lived and died without ever going far from home. So, the travelling done by my characters would have been considered odd, if not extraordinary.

Lost in a myth of insane medicine, the physicians of the day practiced ridiculous methods. Fevers and deaths, like that of Elizabeth's brother, were common, and often due more to the ignorance of the physician, than to the disease. In the case of Alice Fitton's sudden fever, the choice not to bleed her, would have been considered as ignorant as withholding medicine today would be. The people of the Dark Ages assumed that every infection began in the blood, and the more blood you could draw, the healthier your patient would become. More often than not, it killed them. As a side note, the Black Death, or Bubonic Plague, a disease caused by rat fleas that wiped out approximately one third of the population, would have occurred little more than a generation before, between 1348 and 1349, and would have been each one of these characters' greatest fears.

The writing equipment of the day would have included a quill pen, a bottle of ink, and pieces of cloth or paper. Cloth was used because parchment was so expensive. Though creating paper from trees today is often looked down upon, it was nothing compared to its medieval substitute; animal skins. Parchment was manufactured much like leather. The animal pelts were soaked, "de-haired", and stretched in a place known as a tannery, an institution which had need of being established on the "down wind" side of town.

Though many fiction authors prefer to create their own village for a setting, the town in which my characters are said to have lived is a real. Tonbridge, known in its day as *Tunbridge*, is just thirty miles southeast of London.

I didn't use excerpts from the Wycliffe Bible because of the Old English being so hard to obtain and understand. Neither did I substitute it with a more common translation. The reason being that the Latin Vulgate was later discovered later to have flaws, which is why modern translators defer to the Greek, Hebrew, and Aramaic.

Most of us have grown up with the Scriptures readily accessible to us. There are Bibles at every bookstore, in most hotel nightstands, and available as apps for our cell phones. This is a liberty we enjoy as free citizens, but just like any other freedom, it wasn't free at all. It cost quite a bit, in fact. Translating the Scriptures into English was a war that was waged for centuries. Historians will cite different reasons for this, but the truth of the matter is this; the Holy Church had generations living and dying in fear. To hand them the truth would have been like handing the keys to a chained slave. The people, too ignorant to understand that they were being manipulated, did whatever the Church asked of them. The Word of God is a powerful thing. The clergy knew this better than anyone. Only a few scholars like John Wycliffe, William Tyndale, and Martin Luther saw the people's need for God and took action. It was a high price. Men and women gave their lives for this cause because they knew its value. They knew that no other book in the world, as enlightening or exciting as it might have been, had the power to change lives like the Holy Bible. There is no end to what the Word of God can do. It can transform broken people. It can set free the prisoners of fear, and we, just like the characters in this story, have been entrusted with it. So, what will we do? Someone has to tell them. Someone has to set them free.

> "But as we have been approved by God
> to be entrusted with the gospel,
> even so we speak
> Not as pleasing men, but God Who tests our hearts."
> ~1 Thessalonians 2:4 NKJV

CPSIA information can be obtained at www.ICGtesting.com
Printed in the USA
BVOW011612280213

314424BV00001B/83/P